IN SEARCH OF AN IDENTITY

By M.W. Burdette

ISBN-10: 0-9971553-0-2
ISBN-13: 978-09971553-0-3

This is a work of fiction. Names, characters, businesses, places, events and incidents are either the products of the author's imagination or used in a fictitious manner. Any resemblance to actual persons, living or dead, or actual events is purely coincidental.

Original Publication Date: January, 2016. Published in the United States of America by Amazon.com.

DEDICATION

This book is dedicated to my original editor and loving wife, Dr. Martha Bruner Burdette. Besides putting up with my quirks for many years, she has been an inspiration to everyone with her unlimited work effort, kindness to others, and her desire to make the world a better place in which to live.

CONTENTS

INTRODUCTION

PART I: CONFLICT IN SOUTHEAST ASIA
1. A Calculating Mind
2. Chaos in Hue
3. Saigon, 1968
4. Magic Fingers Steam and Cream Massage Parlor
5. Colonel J.P. Forsett
6. Discovering the Leak in S-2
7. An Unexpected R&R to Bangkok!
8. The Calm before the Storm
9. Goodbye Subic Bay, Hello Saigon!
10. I Need a Drink!
11. Klahan Goes Undercover
12. Enticing Lieutenant Bremen to the Massage Parlor
13. Klahan Takes John to Forsett's Office
14. Introducing Bill Hicks
15. Developing a Plan
16. Bill Hicks Meets Tuyen and Her Girls
17. Bill Hicks of the GAO
18. An Untimely Visit from a Senator
19. The Four Suspects Identified
20. Looks Can Be Deceiving
21. A Captain and a Major
22. Major Beckers
23. Tu Thi Da'o
24. Making the Best of a Bad Situation
25. The Traitor Is Exposed

PART II: A MAN ON THE RUN
26. All Good Things Must End

27. Planning for the Big Exit
28. An Evasive Sergeant Major in Bangkok
29. The Great Escape
30. Sergeant Almandinger
31. Cousin Jimmy the Hoodlum
32. Setting a Trap for Briggs
33. Getting Closure for Tuyen
34. Briggs in Kumamoto
35. Briggs Makes a Major Miscalculation
36. To Catch a Traitor, You Need to Be Sneaky
37. Money Greases the Wheels of Justice

PART III: A MOVING TARGET
38. I Am Alive and Living in Japan
39. A Boat Ride to Kumamoto
40. A Quick Trip to Seoul
41. A Big Needle in a Small Haystack
42. Dallas is a Civilized City
43. Tracing a Traitor
44. The Tokyo CIA
45. The Senator's Hands Are Not Clean
46. Tightening the Noose
47. The Senator and the Traitor
48. How to Catch a Thief
49. Politics and Powerful Weapons
50. The Slippery Sergeant Major Briggs
51. A Tricky Trap in Nassau
52. Changing Base of Operations

PART IV: CLOSING IN ON THE PREY
53. There's No Place Like Home
54. Missing in Action
55. Southern California is the Place to Live
56. The Secret to Shipping M-16 Assault Rifles
57. How to Trace the Untraceable

58. The Dallas Crime Family Hierarchy
59. A Move from Saigon to Dallas
60. Tuning in on the Crime Syndicate
61. It's Time to Move Some Weapons
62. Jimmy Garrison's Place in the Family
63. The Senator Is Dead
64. Putting It All Together
65. Tuyen Is Happy in Dallas
66. Let the Raid Begin!
67. Picking up Briggs' Trail Again

EPILOGUE

PART I: CONFLICT IN SOUTHEAST ASIA

Chapter 1

A Calculating Mind

"If you ever go to Vegas," Lieutenant JG Bill Nelson said, "they're going to break your fingers for counting cards! Really, John, how in the hell do you do that? I've seen some card counters in the past, but you take the cake."

"It's a gift," John answered with a slight smile. "Algebra, chemistry, physics, statistics...they all came to me real easy. I never cracked a book to study for a quiz; I just remember what I see. Even foreign languages are so structured that they are pretty easy for me, too. However, don't ask me about English composition!" He laughed as he put down a straight flush and took the poker pot for the fifth time in a row. They were sitting in the Officer's Club on Subic Bay with a view of the cascading ocean in the distance. The ceiling-to-floor windows provided a breathtaking view of this tropical paradise in the Philippines.

"OK, smart guy, how many languages do you speak, read or understand?"

"Let's see," he thought for a minute with his finger and thumb to his chin for effect, "Chinese, French, Spanish, Vietnamese, Portuguese, Japanese, Swahili, and, of course, English."

"Damn, boy, you're a walking linguist!"

"Well, it comes in handy in Mexican, Chinese, French, Vietnamese or Japanese restaurants. You can hear what the waiters and servers are saying about you when you leave your tip!" He roared with a belly laugh, humoring himself with the answer.

"So, how would you ask a beautiful Vietnamese girl to go to bed with you, assuming you had the chance to do so?"

"Baby-san," John played along, "you want to fucky-fucky for ten dollar bill?" he answered and gave Nelson an unassuming look.

"Right, you asshole. You just never can give me a straight answer on anything, can you?"

"Hey, you asked me, and I told you—what more do you want?"

"Fuck you, Bremen. You are a maniac!"

"So why did you take so many foreign languages in school anyway? What university did you attend back in the good old USA?"

"Now that's a shaggy-dog story in itself. My mom wanted me to be an engineer because my older brother was an engineer. I thought she was going to disown me when I registered at Ashburn University just north of Birmingham, Alabama. It had about 2500 students—the ratio of women to men was seven to one! Need I say more?"

"Was your brother successful? Was that why she wanted you to follow in his footsteps?"

"Nah, she just thought my liberal arts education was a waste of money. She meant well, but there's no way in hell I wanted to turn out like my brother. I hate to talk unkindly about my family, but he was a loser from day one. By the time I had graduated from college, he had already been married three times and bankrupt twice. My brother Joe was so smart he even threatened the I.R.S.! You can see why I wanted to go the other way."

John had a slender, muscular build, hazel eyes, sandy brown hair, and a lean and hungry look. He was five-feet-eleven inches standing barefoot, and there wasn't an ounce of fat on his body. He had been a tennis player in college and was proud of his slim appearance.

"So, if you didn't want to be an engineer, what was your goal when you graduated? With all of those languages, you could be a teacher or a professor with advanced degrees."

"I'm going to be a lawyer and join my Uncle Chad's law firm in Birmingham once I am free of my military obligation. He's saving a place for me."

"Well, you got a lucky break getting assigned to Subic Bay instead of Vietnam. How did you pull that off?"

"I joined for four years instead of taking my chances on being drafted and winding up a 'ground-pounder' like a lot of my college friends who were drafted right out of college. I was promised a duty assignment that was not in Vietnam. How did you manage to stay out of 'Nam?"

LT JG Nelson said with a little smile, "My dad is a three-star general back in Washington. Having a father who is a big shot officer in the Pentagon can come in handy."

"Well, good for you, Nelson. It's a shame anyone has to fight a war in a country where no one wants us. What a bummer!"

"It's also a shame that you're no good at poker," John said, sipping on his Johnny Walker Black and raking in Bill's money.

Chapter 2

Chaos in Hue

Tran Klahan Chu was born in Hue and grew up in chaos. His entire life was spent trying to emulate his parents, who were educated in Hue and taught at Hue University. He followed in their footsteps with his early education at a Catholic day school, followed by his successful entry into Hue University in the spring of 1967. Just as he was completing his second year at the university in early 1968, the Tet Offensive became a reality to everyone living in the former capital of Vietnam. Hue University was in flames, Klahan's parents and siblings were missing and presumed dead, and he was hiding in a makeshift bunker constructed of concrete normally used in drainage line construction.

Terrified and horrified, Klahan could not believe this could happen to law abiding people. It shattered his belief system and had an irreversible effect on his outlook for the future in his beloved homeland. Once known as a lovely French province, Hue had become a burnt and bombed-out remnant of civilization. It was more than Klahan could handle, and he planned to move to Saigon to join with the forces battling the Viet Cong and the NVA. His destiny was set that January morning in 1968, and he would never look back.

Klahan took the meager belongings salvaged from the destruction of his home and village and set out for Saigon. The Viet Cong had burned his house to the ground, along with every other house on his street. He was walking down Highway 1, with his mind in a fog.

"And where are you going, young lady?" Klahan said to a very pretty young girl named Nguyen Tuyen Chung. He had overtaken her on the road to Saigon.

"My family was killed in the attack at Hue, and I have been left orphaned by the Viet Cong," she lamented. Tuyen had lived in Hue with her father, who had worked for the municipal government. He and her mother were executed in front of her when the city was overrun. Looking at them standing side by side, Klahan towered over her since she was so short in stature. "I don't know why I was spared when they were murdered," she wailed to Klahan. It was obvious to him that her spirit was broken. "I have been living day to day, scavenging where I can for something to eat and a safe place to sleep."

After learning her story, Klahan took one long look at Tuyen and knew that they must work together to honor their parents and seek revenge on the murderous Viet Cong who had taken everything away from them in Hue.

"How will we go about honoring them, Klahan? We are but two insignificant young people with no weapons or connections to people in power," said Tuyen.

"Do not worry, little angel. We have the greatest weapon of all. We have justification to avenge our parents' deaths. We will, somehow, do this for them and our families!" Klahan responded, and he swore on the memory of his parents that he would find a way to do that. As this point, he did not know when or how he would be able to avenge the loss of his family, but he would not rest until he was able to honor that vow.

*   *   *   *   *

It was no small chore getting from Hue to Saigon with no money, no transportation and nothing but sheer determination to keep them moving southward toward their ultimate goal. It was over 390 miles to Saigon, and after a week of scavenging and begging for rides south, they had only reached Da Nang. There had to be a better way of achieving their goals than hoofing it all the way to Saigon.

"Tuyen, we need to have a plan that is smarter than walking to Saigon," Klahan said. "I have been hearing from the local elders as we pass through the villages that the American Government is looking for educated local Vietnamese girls and young men to help staff their buildings and work as houseboys and house girls. How much education do you have?" he asked, hoping that she was not illiterate.

"I finished high school at a Catholic mission in Hue, but I have heard that the house girls for the American G.I.s are concubines. I don't know if I can do that," she whispered in a little girl voice. "I would be too embarrassed to be a Geisha Girl!"

"No, no, Tuyen. I understand that it is not permitted for the house girls on an American base to even touch an American soldier or to have any romantic relationship with anyone on their bases." This thought also began playing in Klahan's brain, as he began formulating a plan to make this work for both of them.

"I think we can get a ride to Saigon if we tell them that we are going to be working on an American base. We will tell them that we are brother and sister and that we cannot be separated. That way, I can look out for you when we get to Saigon," he stated confidently. Actually, Klahan had no idea if he could pull this rouse off, but it sure was worth a try.

Flagging down a MACV 5 ton truck, Klahan told his story to the driver, who had little or no interest in helping. Six attempts later, he was able to convince a young Marine from Idaho to let them ride to Saigon with him in his truck. He was on the way to Long Binh, the major supply depot for the Americans in the southern part of Vietnam. They covered more distance in six hours in the back of the supply truck than they had covered in the prior week. The bread, peanut butter and beer that they found in the truck were unexpected treats. Things were looking up for Klahan and Tuyen.

Chapter 3

Saigon, 1968

The US Military Assistance Command Vietnam, or MACV, was headquartered just adjacent to the Tan Son Nhut Airport, just north of the city of Saigon. Originally established in the Cholon area of central Saigon, it was relocated when it outgrew the facilities. All of the military operations in Vietnam were controlled by MACV, and its influence over all other support services was evident. The MACV compound and ARVN headquarter were sharing some of the same building space near the big air base.

Klahan and Tuyen needed a big break to be able to get established in Saigon. Klahan had spoken to some of the other local residents who were working on the big air base and in the other US Government establishments in and around Saigon. He was able to get Tuyen a job working as a hooch maid in a security compound near the base. She was happy that she had not had to go to work in a bar or massage parlor.

Klahan was eventually hired as a driver for the MACV Sergeant Major Daniel Briggs. Briggs was the highest ranking enlisted man in the country of Vietnam, and he wielded great influence in both US Government circles and local ARVN circles of power. Briggs was a short man, no more than 5' 8" tall, and pudgy. His G.I. haircut was cut so close that Klahan could count the freckles on the sides of his head. His starched uniform would stand up on its own if removed from his body. Briggs had grown up near Dallas, Texas, and he had been in a little trouble for rowdy behavior with the law from time to time. He had some relatives who were on the national crime watch list. Deciding to steer clear of those potential troublemakers, Briggs had joined the US Army when he was only seventeen years old, and he had never returned to Dallas.

This was an intense, no-nonsense man whose presence alone could strike fear into the toughest of combat-hardened men. His eyes were dark as dirty rice paddies, and his gait authoritative. Klahan liked him immediately.

Briggs appreciated having a well-educated driver who could help him decipher the motivation and language of the local Vietnamese. Klahan soon became a very important confidant for Briggs, a position instrumental in Klahan's rise to power in the local Saigon area. Klahan was excited to tell Tuyen about the job that he hoped would help them reach their ultimate goals of revenge. Klahan knew that he would have to endear himself to Briggs to get the intelligence he needed about the Battle of Hue. Klahan had to come up with a plan to tie himself to Briggs that he would not question. He had to make Briggs dependent on his knowledge and expertise of Vietnamese customs and practices.

*   *   *   *   *

"We need to get more involved with the Americans so we can find out who was responsible for the loss of our village and the death of our families," Klahan told Tuyen. "There must be a way to see what the Americans have in their battle history accounts of the destruction of Hue. We will never be able to find out what really happened until we are able to see who and why our parents were targeted for death by the NVA and the Viet Cong."

"And just how do you plan to do that, Klahan? Do you think you can just go up to an American general and ask him your questions and believe that he will give you an honest answer?" She giggled when she said this because she knew that would be a foolhardy gesture.

"I have an idea that I think will work, but it will require a lot of you, and I'm not sure you will want to do what is required," Klahan said with a bit of disappointment in his voice. "Sometimes it takes great sacrifices to get justice!"

"I am willing to do whatever is necessary to avenge my family's murders. What could be a bigger sacrifice than them giving their lives for what they believed in and held dear to their hearts?" Tuyen replied with a true tone of conviction in her voice.

Klahan thought before he made his suggestion very tactfully, concerned that she might give up on getting back at the hated NVA and Viet Cong. He not only wanted a partner is this endeavor; he needed a partner who would see this through to the end.

"Tuyen, I have heard that the Americans will pay gladly for the comfort of a woman, and that they speak openly about the war when they are happy and satisfied," Klahan said, almost in a soft whisper. "You are a beautiful young woman, and it would be easy for you to have the soldier of your choice, assuming you still want to pursue this plan. I will understand if you decide that it is too much of a sacrifice."

"I would give my very own life to avenge my family," she said quietly. "Nothing is too much to make their killers pay! But how can we make sure I will find the right American with the information that we need?"

"Don't worry, Tuyen, because I will be your partner in this endeavor. I have begun to make friends, and I have connections with the American forces that can help us decide whom to target."

"I trust you like a brother, Klahan," she said and hugged him tightly.

Chapter 4

Magic Fingers Steam and Cream Massage Parlor

Tuyen was as smart as she was beautiful. 4-feet-9 inches tall and weighing 90 pounds, Tuyen might initially be mistaken for an easy pushover, but she was like dynamite or C4 plastic explosives – a big problem when not handled correctly. Although she had only finished high school at the Catholic school before she was so cruelly dispatched into the world with the fall of Hue, Tuyen could have excelled in any field of endeavor she might have chosen. Now her field of study was the reality of war and how she could use that situation to reach her ultimate goal of taking down the individuals who had killed her precious family. A stroke of luck had teamed her with Klahan after the destruction of Hue. He would use her to achieve his goals, but she would return the favor.

"I need a better plan if I am going to reach my goals of finding out who killed my family," Tuyen thought to herself as she keep playing out different scenarios in her head. She was only one, insignificant person trying to find information that was most likely hidden in confidential files somewhere in the NVA or American Governments' documents recounting the battle of Hue. So, she did the only thing possible at the time. She confided in Klahan that she wanted to get more involved in the plan to find the bastards who had killed her family and bring them to justice, but not the kind of justice that might or might not find the murderers guilty of some war crime with a legal system to protect them in the long run. No, she was talking about an AK-47 type of justice, and she was willing to be the judge, jury, and executioner when the time came to make those decisions.

"Klahan," she said, "what we need is more than just one or two of us trying to find the mastermind of the plan to destroy our families and the city of Hue." No, what we need is a network of people who are sympathetic to our cause and who may have lost loved ones in the destruction of Hue. I think I have a plan that will help us get to that end."

"Really?" Klahan looked curiously and surprisingly at Tuyen with a slight grin. "So, out of the mouth of babes comes the solution to all of our problems."

"I am deadly serious," she said with conviction and some irritation. "You have your ways of fighting the NVA and Viet Cong, and I have my ways."

"And just what are those ways, little jewel, that will get us the information and put us in the position to bring justice to the loss of our families?" He really didn't believe a young, seventeen-year-old girl who had little knowledge of the world, much less of war, could come up with a reasonable plan that would actually help them achieve their goals of ultimate revenge. But, he would be willing to hear her out.

"The American G.I. likes young, Vietnamese women and will spend lots of their money on them to be pleasured and forget that they are in a war that they don't want to be in, right? The way I see it is that all we have to do is recruit other young Vietnamese women who are also abandoned or lost to this war and who will be willing to help us get the information we need from these G.I.s. What we need to figure out is how to get them to agree to help us. There has to be something in it for them, besides the money that they will surely get from the men with whom they have sex. There has to be something else—a club or organization that ties us all together for the greater good."

"Go on," Klahan said.

She paused, formulated more of her thoughts and continued. "Since you have been working in the SGT Major's office on base, have you been able to find out any information that would help locate other families from Hue that suffered the same type of personal injustice that we did? If we could find other young women who would be willing to sacrifice their personal lives and compromise themselves for the same cause, we could build a brothel that could be an information outlet for our cause."

"And what do you think we should name this massage parlor, Tuyen?"

"Magic Fingers Steam and Cream Massage Parlor?" she said with a little giggle. "I think the more ridiculous the name, the better our chances to operate under the noses of the Americans without them getting wind of our plan."

"OK, I know several Americans who work in an intelligence agency who have access to everything that goes on in the country south of the DMZ. And, " Klahan said with some satisfaction as his plan was taking shape, "the name you have chosen is excellent!"

Klahan knew that everything that happened south of the DMZ would eventually pass through the MACV S-2 Section, and Klahan had been making friends with many of the guys who worked in that particular section of the command. At first he was just another young Vietnamese national trying to get by and make conversation with his new friends. However, in just a few days' time he was having lunch with them and sharing war stories that kept them on the edge of their seats.

Klahan was a good storyteller, and he planned to use those skills to endear himself to as many Americans as possible. The DMZ, or Demilitarized Zone, was a narrow band of land just south of the 17th parallel North of latitude, separating North Vietnam from South Vietnam. Heavy fighting was always breaking out in and near this area. Although the American Forces were suspected of having counter surveillance teams that infiltrated the north through this area, most of the American effort was concentrated on helping the ARVN and the South Vietnamese Government resist and defend the major cities of Hue, Da Nang, Bien Hue, Vung Tau, and Saigon.

He had initially thought that his best way to get information from MACV would be to infiltrate the office and smuggle that information out without being caught. However, now that Tuyen had shared her thoughts about linking up other displaced young

Vietnamese women with their cause, it gave Klahan another idea. In Saigon alone, there were many massage parlors where the soldiers could get stoned and laid without walking very far off any military compound. These havens of sin were lined up like the used car lots outside the Army base on Victory Drive in Columbus, Georgia. It wasn't that you couldn't find what you wanted on almost any used car lot; the question was whether you were willing to pay to play. Nothing different here in Saigon, except instead of buying a used car, the horny jarhead was renting a beautiful china doll for a few minutes or hours. It all came down to whether he thought the deal was worth the money or not.

Klahan simply could hire the right hand-picked girls, teach them what information that he wanted them to get from the soldiers, and then compile all of that intelligence information into a useable form. Of course, there were some wrinkles to work out, but he'd be damned if he didn't think that the plan would work.

"Tuyen," he asked, "can you get some of the other locals that work in the enlisted men's clubs as waitresses and some of the other house girls to identify other abandoned girls that have come here from Hue without a way to take care of themselves? I'm sure there are many who have had the same things happen to them."

"Well," she said. "I can begin to ask them and see if they know of anyone. But, how we will convince them to join us in our plan?"

"Just get me their names, and I will do the rest."

"I will start today," she called cheerfully as she left for work at the massive Tan Son Nhut Airbase. She had been working as a house girl now for several weeks and had begun to get acquainted with many of the soldiers who either lived there or worked nearby. Lovely as she was, she had an endless number of guys asking her out on dates, or blatantly just asking her to sleep with them. She had always demurely and shyly just continued her work without letting them know that she had either heard or understood them, but she read, spoke and understood English very well. Now, she would do the opposite – get them to spend their money on her to advance her plan.

Chapter 5

Colonel J.P. Forsett

Colonel Justice P. Forsett, or J.P. to his inner circle, was a formidable looking man at six-feet-and-three-inches, and although in his mid-40's, he was still in excellent physical shape. He had a military haircut and a couple of cannons for arms. He was a true Southern gentleman, according to all reports, and he spoke with a pronounced accent.

Colonel Forsett also had a big problem. Somewhere, somehow, information was leaking out of his S-2 Section like a sinking ship. What didn't make sense was that there were no local Vietnamese Nationals working inside the departments where classified material was produced, disseminated, and stored. So that meant that his people were leaking the information. In a war zone, such an offense is paramount to treason and could actually be dealt with in-country. If he caught the bastard, that lousy son-of-a-bitch would disappear altogether. But first, he had to catch him or them!

On top of that problem, the CIA had informed the S-2 in Washington that Chinese-made AK-47 rifles had been detected in the San Francisco area, and they were now being distributed by the crime families all over the US. It was apparent to the top brass that this involvement with weapons trafficking was probably tied to the information leaks and other criminal activities stemming from the security breach in Saigon. This channel for the American crime families must be detected and stopped before war broke out on the streets of American cities. This new knowledge led the colonel to a decision that could endanger his command and land him in Ft. Leavenworth, but he could no longer turn a blind eye to the situation happening under his nose here in Saigon. He had to come up with a comprehensive plan to find and stop the leak.

At first he thought that it wouldn't be hard to find out who had been the culprit, but the task had become much harder than he had expected. And, it wasn't a matter of the rights of his men or any crap like that that held the colonel back from discovering the asshole who had cost them both battle victories and the lives of some of his men. The traitor was simply smarter than hell. He knew he would finally catch him, but it was frustrating not being able to do it quickly. He needed a better plan, and he thought he might try something a little outside the box to jump start his investigation.

Colonel Forsett had noticed that Briggs had been using a Vietnamese national to do his driving in and around Saigon. Forsett had been impressed with the young man because he was fluent in English, well-mannered and seemed to be very intelligent and knowledgeable about the Saigon area. Briggs told Forsett that he had hired Klahan for two reasons. First, he was a sharp, young man with above average intelligence and knew when to speak and when to listen. And, second, Klahan hated the NVA and Viet Cong more than any American could ever hate them. Klahan had shared how he and his sister Tuyen had been robbed of their parents and other family members by the murderous Viet Cong. There was little or no danger that this young Vietnamese national was going to aid and abet the enemy for any reason whatsoever.

Forsett called out to the duty sergeant, "Sergeant Thomas, get me SGT Major Briggs on the horn. Now!"

"Yes, sir," Thomas said, dialing the SGT Major's office number.

"Briggs, here," he answered in a clipped voice.

"SGT Major Briggs, Colonel Forsett would like a word with you."

"Put him on," the gruff voice of Briggs called back to Thomas.

"Please hold for Colonel Forsett." It seemed to take an excessive amount of time before Briggs heard the familiar voice of Colonel Forsett on the line.

16

"Daniel, this is J.P. I have a problem that I don't want to discuss over the phone lines. How does your afternoon look?"

Briggs answered, "Tell me what time do you want me there, sir, and I will make it happen."

"The sooner the better. Why don't you come over around 1800 hours and let's get some chow and talk a bit?"

"Absolutely, sir," he replied. "See you then."

"Oh, and by the way, bring that young Vietnamese local driver with you to the meeting."

"Yes, sir."

Now, it wasn't unusual for the colonel to summon his top NCO over for a conference, but this situation seemed a little different to Briggs. Forsett had never instructed him to bring any other enlisted man with him to one of these meetings, let alone, a Vietnamese national. He had been in this man's Army long enough to spot irregular movements from the brass, and he was sure that he would find out soon enough what it was all about. After twenty-two years in the Army, he had learned long ago not to question orders from his officers. He just did the smart thing and followed orders.

*　*　*　*　*

When Briggs arrived, Klahan let him out in front of the building and began to pull the jeep away from the curb.

"Hold it there, Klahan," Briggs called to him. "I'm going to need you to go inside with me this time."

Klahan was stupefied. "Are you sure, SGT Major?"

Briggs was not used to anyone, let alone a local foreign national, questioning his commands. However, he did not blast the young man, but rather simply said to him in a firm but civil tone, "Your guess about this is as good as mine." Briggs walked into the facility, with Klahan close behind.

As they approached his office, Briggs opened the door, went up to his desk and saluted the colonel in military fashion. Klahan stood alongside the sergeant major, not really knowing what to do. The colonel returned Brigg's salute crisply and then put them both at ease by asking them to take a seat in the chairs directly across from his gigantic mahogany desk. Briggs kept thinking to himself, "How in the hell did he get that impressive desk over here?" However, as good protocol demanded, he did not venture the question to the colonel.

"Klahan, I believe?" the colonel said and rose to offer a hand of welcome to his young guest. "I'm glad to meet you. I have heard a lot of good things about you from SGT Major Briggs and the other NCOs at S-2 about your willingness to contribute to the cause down here in Saigon. How did a bright young man such as you get mixed up in all of the stuff going on politically in Saigon right now?"

The colonel paused for a moment to let that question get some purchase on Klahan's thoughts. He knew that there had to be more to the story than that of a misplaced youth in a war zone. This kid was too smart and too sharp to just happen to be anywhere, much less on an American military base.

The colonel went on, "So, just exactly how did that happen?"

Klahan gave some thoughtful consideration to the question and then answered. "Colonel Forsett, I am going to be totally honest with you. I am here on a mission to find those responsible for the attack on my family in Hue, and I intend to bring them to justice for their war crimes. I know that may sound strange coming from a driver for an American NCO, but that is my eventual goal. I have a younger sister with me, and she and I are both dedicated to our cause, and we will stop at nothing to reach this goal of revenging the loss of our family to the NVA and Viet Cong insurgents."

Klahan sat back in his chair and waited for the answer that he was sure the colonel would give him.

"You can't take the law into your own hands; you can't rely on vigilante justice; you can't be judge, jury and executioner all at the same time," the colonel predictably said.

18

However, Klahan was totally surprised when the colonel asked him, "So, are you interested in a partner to help you accomplish this goal? If that is what you would like to happen, we may be able to help each other to our mutual profit and satisfaction."

"What did you have in mind, sir?" Klahan asked with a genuine desire to know if this military man could help him with his goals. "I have some thoughts in mind, but you are obviously much wiser than I am."

"Klahan, you have my honest and true word that I will not reveal anything about your plan as long as it does not endanger any US Troops. I hate those NVA and Viet Cong bastards as much as you, but my hands are tied to using certain available technological tools that could enhance our chances of getting to the bottom of this situation."

Klahan figured where the colonel was going with this information and beat him to the finish line.

"So, if I understand you, sir, you would like to make a deal with me and those who work with me to exchange information? Is that what you are implying, sir?" Klahan tactfully put his question to the colonel.

The colonel simply nodded and glanced at Briggs with a knowing stare. It was evident that there must be some give and take to make such a deal advantageous to both sides.

"Yes, Klahan, I am asking you to become an undercover person for me in certain situations to help us determine who in my own outfit is leaking information to the enemy and why they are doing it. For that information, we can assist you and your sister with money for lodging, food, and other niceties."

"And what I want and what I need is information on the Battle at Hue and why our family was singled out for destruction by the Viet Cong and NVA. You might say information for information, sir."

"So, if I can get you some tangible information on how and why your family was slaughtered, you will help us find our information leak?"

"Absolutely, sir, just tell me what you want me to do."

"Klahan, will you please excuse me and SGT Major Briggs for a moment? We need to discuss some other private business, and then I will begin to tell you how I think we can help you and tell you what you need to do for us," the colonel said matter of factly.

"Sure, sir, I will be in the outer office," Klahan said. He rose and left the room, closing the door behind him as he departed the room.

"Daniel," the colonel directly addressed Briggs, now with a renewed intensity once the outer door to his office had been closed. "I think we may finally be able to get something going here that could dramatically impact our success in this lousy country. I'm thinking that we need to take the bull by the horns and get a grip on this information leak once and for all. I want it stopped, and I want it stopped now!" he roared.

Briggs, not to appear dominated by Forsett, simply nodded in the affirmative. "How do you want to play this, Colonel?"

"Give me until tomorrow around 1500 hours and report back to me without Klahan, and we will put a plan together."

"Yes, sir," Briggs replied, saluting the colonel. He left the colonel's office for his own office, with Klahan in tow.

Chapter 6

Discovering the Leak in S-2

The next day, the colonel met with Briggs, and they did some strategic planning for the project with the sergeant's young Vietnamese jeep driver. They knew that he would ask information of them that they really had no authority to give without a direct order from the director of S-2 in Washington, but, after all, this was a war zone, and some decisions had to be made without all of the back and forth negotiating that normally took place when Washington got involved in any decision-making process. They would cross that bridge when they had to and not regret it for a millisecond.

"So, Daniel," the colonel started, "have you thought how we might use Klahan to further our goal of finding the leak that's contributing to so many deaths and failures in the field of battle?"

Scratching his somewhat receding hairline absentmindedly, Briggs said, "Well, sir, I know this for sure. Klahan and his sister were both robbed of their entire family, and they are hell-bent on revenge. I think we can use that information as a catalyst to get them to work actively for us. All we will need to do is to leak some information ourselves on some of the details of the Battle of Hue, and their cooperation will know no bounds."

"Hmmnn," the colonel paused to consider what his top NCO had shared with him. "You know, Daniel, we could use this situation to bolster our relationship with the ARVN Headquarters as well if we play our cards right."

"How so, sir?" Briggs knew that the ARVN Military Command was suspicious of the MACV Alliance, and it definitely could use some warming up if there was a way to accomplish that without flagrantly breaking the law or committing some traitorous act.

The colonel continued, "When you left yesterday, I did a little research on my own, and I think I have come up with a pretty achievable plan to turn this theft of intelligence into a major gain for us. We need to infiltrate our own ranks with a deep cover operative so above suspicion that even he will not know the complete details of his mission until he is in country and on board with us. The plan must be set into motion subtly and appear to unfold in its own time for it to work without the S.O.B. who is leaking the info to get wind of it. It's obviously someone at the command level who has coordinates of our planned incursions and battle plans. 'Charlie' just knows too much to be picking this stuff up over the airwaves."

"You know, Daniel, the way the Viet Cong got their name is quite a story in itself. A Korean officer told me that 'Charlie' was one of the more respectable nicknames given to the Viet Cong insurgents who were causing most of the sapper explosions and midnight raids on the villagers who had cooperated with the American forces. It was still considered a racial slur, but it was derived by the Koreans by shortening the name of the Viet Cong forces to the VC. The NATO phonetic alphabet is pronounced 'Victor-Charlie,' which was shortened even more to 'Charlie' by the front line forces as they encountered and fought them in the jungle. Now if you want to believe that story, and I don't know why you wouldn't, it makes sense why some of the other handles like 'Sir Charles,' 'Mr. Charles,' and 'Chuck' were also used to refer to the little buggers!" the colonel finished with a bit of a laugh.

"But back to the matter at hand, Briggs. This young Vietnamese man you are using for your driver seems to be the kind of person who can pull off my plan of infiltrating our cadre of troops, yes?"

"Yes, sir."

"After you left last night, I contacted a personal friend of mine at the Pentagon, General Nelson, who just happens to be assigned to the S-2 section. He has a son at Subic Bay, and the kid is a hell-raiser, to say the least. It just happens that his kid is a Lieutenant

JG and good friends with a Lieutenant John Bremen, who is simply marking his time until he can get out and get involved in his family's law practice. Bremen has language skills that may be helpful to us in finding this damn traitor who is leaking all of our secret information all over Indo-China. This LT Bremen speaks several languages, including Swahili, and he is wasting his enlistment hiding out at Subic Bay, just waiting for his term of service to expire. According to one of his pals over there, he has an almost eidetic memory. He could really help us in our search to find and seal the intelligence leak that we have here at MACV. He signed some deal with the Navy to be able to choose his duty station if he signed up for four years. The way around this is to let him get his first duty station and then move him on a temporary basis until we can reassign him permanently here. A little shady move, I admit, but not an illegal one."

Briggs nodded.

The colonel seemed to be reenergizing himself as he relayed his plan. "So I called the general and asked him if he could encourage his son to invite Lieutenant Bremen to take an R&R in Bangkok. He said he could make it happen. So, the plan has been put into motion, and we need to work it from our end now. Let's give this a couple of weeks to materialize, and then we will move forward with the details."

Briggs was beginning to marvel at Forsett's strategy. He was a fucking genius. "I like it, sir," Briggs said. "I like it a lot!"

Forsett went on, "What we have to do, Daniel, is get Klahan to Bangkok and have him bump into Lieutenant Bremen and strike up a relationship with him while he is there on his R&R. I have a good suspicion that Klahan won't need a lot of coaching on how to make that happen," he said with a hearty laugh. "The kid is simply smarter than shit! Bremen will not even see it coming. How soon can we get him over there on a MAC flight, so we don't have to show him on a manifest? I don't want to show our hand to anyone, since we have no idea who the bad apple is."

"I'll check with the dispatcher out at Tan Son Nhut, who owes me a couple of favors. We should be able to make that happen within the two-week time frame that it will take to get Bremen to Bangkok with the general's son, sir," Briggs said. "As far as the flight crew will know, Klahan will look like just another duffle bag."

"Okay, Top. Make it happen!"

Chapter 7

An Unexpected R&R to Bangkok!

Bill Nelson sat down beside John and began to strike up a conversation about the opportunities for entertainment and recreation near the mammoth base. Both of them had visited the Cockeyed Cowboy and the Blow Heaven Bar with similar results—a nice hangover in the morning and quite a few less Pisos in their pockets. The evening visits to these clubs were simply vague memories to help lonely American servicemen weather the long time away from home and friends. The trick was to figure out how to have a wild evening of drinking and other pleasures without being hauled in by the SPs.

It wasn't a good idea to tempt fate and become an item of interest to the brass who could change one's orders for a patrol boat on the Mekong River in the blink of the eye. No, one had to be clever to stay in the background of this hellish war and remain alive. So far, John had managed to do just that. He was not a poster child for the innocent, but he had managed to fly below the radar and felt quite happy about his accomplishments.

"Hey, John. I hear that there are some opportunities to visit Thailand on an R&R and that the women are simply gorgeous. China dolls with no inhibitions. Are you up for some cultural stimulation?"

Nelson was one of those 'pretty boys' who could have modeled for a magazine and received top money for his time. Everyone knew that he was the son of a general, and his short tour of duty in the Navy had been greased all the way from college to Subic Bay. The brass understood that he was to be ignored when it came to bending a few rules, and unless he was doing something that could be considered to be treasonous, it was just better to turn a blind eye to his antics. John has been on a few local barhopping trips with Nelson in the past, so it appeared to him that as long as he was with this junior officer, he would probably be able to steer clear of too much trouble, and yet, still have a pretty good time.

"Sounds like a good idea to me!" Within a two-week span, he and Bill had booked a Rest and Recuperation leave to Bangkok with reservations at New Phetchaburi Road and Jack's All American Star Bar and Thai Heaven. It was deliciously decadent and mind-numbingly effective in forgetting the war.

The trip was a success for John, and he was relaxed and ready to reassume his boring duties at Subic Bay once he returned. He would have preferred to remain in Bangkok for the duration of his overseas duty, but that was not possible.

He was dreading the return to Subic Bay the next morning when a local, well-dressed Vietnamese gentleman sat down on a bar stool beside him and struck up a conversation. His name was Klahan, and the conversation turned from bar-girls, to contraband, to the shitty war in Vietnam. This guy was very informed and eager to share all his secrets to success in Thailand's Pitaya district. He boasted of his conquests with the local women and his ability to negotiate the illegal and sensitive ivory trade that made local Thai merchants wealthy.

Having consumed his normal two days' quota of scotch in a matter of three hours, John was ready to bid Klahan goodbye and hustle himself back to the hotel for a few hours of sleep before flying back to Subic Bay. Klahan handed John a business card and insisted that he contact him once he was back in the Philippines.

"Sure," John said, with no intention of ever seeing this guy again. It was an evening to pass the time as he was wrapping up a great holiday in Bangkok. This apparent chance meeting of Klahan, however, would have long lasting effects that John could never have anticipated.

Chapter 8

The Calm Before the Storm

Briggs reported back to Colonel Forsett that the plan had been put into motion by Klahan, and that it was time to get those TDY orders for LT Bremen cut before their good work in Bangkok was for naught.

"So how did your boy pull it off with Bremen?" Forsett asked Briggs at roll call the next day.

Briggs answered with a cocky expression on his face, "We casually introduced Klahan to LT Bremen at a bar, and he took John to some other bars and massage parlors. They supposedly had a good time, and Klahan gained John's trust. So, when Bremen is assigned here on a TDY mission, it will be easy for Klahan to bump into him on the streets of Saigon and set the real plan into motion."

The picture was coming into focus for Briggs. The old man was really on top of his game.

Chapter 9

Goodbye Subic Bay, Hello Saigon!

John resumed his routinely boring duties when he returned to Subic Bay and thought nothing more of his encounter with Klahan. He was summoned to Commander Harrison's office about a week after his return to duty from Bangkok. It seemed that he had been given orders for a temporary duty assignment in Saigon for a couple of weeks. No problem. Just enter the country at Cam Ranh Bay, the Navy's large logistic base for incoming material for the war effort, stay a couple of weeks and fly back to Subic Bay when the mission was completed. The only thing he found unsettling about the whole thing was that it seemed to come out of nowhere. But being twenty-three years old and adventurous, he decided to make the best of it.

Arriving at Cam Ranh Bay by sea was quite an experience for a young lieutenant in the Navy. John had read extensively about Vietnam and the 650,000 Americans serving there, but the sheer volume of material being off-loaded was mind boggling. Tanks, trucks, jeeps, endless numbers of containers of food, beer, and other necessities to keep a military presence of this size supplied were beyond his ability to comprehend. "I am in Vietnam now and not in a safe, secluded harbor some 770 nautical miles away. Holy shit!" he thought.

For the first time since he had graduated from college, that little war in Vietnam was very real and very scary. John was hoping his TDY orders would take him to an area that would be in the rear of the action, where he could resume a safe continuation of his military service.

Colonel Forsett had seen to it, however, that John's two-week TDY duties would become a permanent reassignment. John was riding in a Lambretta on his way to The Little White House when he saw a familiar face.

"Klahan? Is that you?" John had to scream to be heard over the noise of the Lambrettas, motorbikes, MACV trucks and other noise pollution that filled the air in Saigon. Amazingly, Klahan pulled alongside John's taxicab and began to explain that he had only been visiting Bangkok on a marketing trip, and now that he was back in Saigon, he was making deals for the ivory and other contraband that he had smuggled into the country. He told John that he had just happened to see John riding by. Saigon was a city of three million people, and the odds of Klahan accidentally bumping into him seemed remote, at best.

Klahan suggested that they stop at a local bar and renew their friendship before John checked into his duty station at the MACV Headquarters in The Little White House compound. Having not seen a friendly face since leaving Subic Bay, John thought it was a good idea.

"What the hell are you doing in this shit-hole, John? I thought you had more sense than to get assigned to 'Nam," Klahan said.

"Well," John replied with a great deal of frustration, "it's not like I volunteered for this duty. Out of a clear blue sky, I received temporary duty orders to come to Saigon to be attached to the MACV Headquarters for a couple of weeks. I figured, what the hell. A little adventure couldn't do me much harm!" Although he laughed nervously, Klahan could see through his bluster that John was full of crap.

"What I want to know," John said to him, "is what the hell YOU are doing here? There must be a more lucrative market for your special sale items than to dogface Army guys and jarheads." All the while, John kept questioning himself. "What were the odds he would simply bump into Klahan some 535 miles from Bangkok?" It was simply too convenient to just be a coincidence.

"So I am guessing that you know the local bars and massage parlors here as well as in Bangkok?" John said.

"Saigon is not quite as unconventional as Bangkok," Klahan replied. "There are two kinds of people in Saigon. Those who would sell their sister to you for two hundred piaster, and those who would kill you for looking at their sister with carnal intent. The trick is to recognize which one is which," he chuckled. "However, I do have a friend who can hook us up with some girls who will show us a good time. Her name is Nguyen Tuyen Chung, and she is connected in Saigon!"

"Bring it on," John said to him. "I feel the need for love, and I want to make the most of my two-week tour of duty in Saigon." This was almost too easy, he thought to himself. He said goodbye to Klahan and carried his gear through the security gates of The Little White House compound.

The Little White House was a secure compound that the Army of South Vietnam, ARVN, used as a base of operations and where the President of South Vietnam, Nguyen Van Thieu, had some of his offices. Thieu had been the VP of South Vietnam before winning the presidential election in 1967, and turned out to be the last president of South Vietnam, as he would abandon the country and leave Saigon a short time before the city fell to the NVA. Actually, no one ever successfully explained to John why the compound was referred to as "The Little White House", since it didn't resemble the US White House at all. The common joke was that it would be harder to fight your way into the Little White House than it would be to defend it from the NVA. John was hoping that was a theory that would go unproven during his two-week stay in Saigon. After all, this was a TDY assignment, and John had no desire to stay more time than his orders required.

"LT Bremen," Colonel Forsett spoke with a commanding Southern accent. "How was your trip over from Subic?"

"This guy is a seriously jacked up and tight-assed dude," thought John. His first opinion of Forsett would not change in the future, as Colonel Forsett appeared to be as consistent as the monsoon rains of Vietnam.

"Fine, sir," John replied confidently. "I would like to ask you a question, though, sir, if you don't mind. I was somewhat surprised to get orders for Saigon for a two-week TDY trip. I just couldn't imagine what could be accomplished in that amount of time in a war zone like Vietnam."

"Yes, about that," the colonel went on in his lazy Southern drawl, "there seems to have been some sort of confusion with the War Department. You have been permanently assigned to me at S-2 here in Saigon. Sorry for the confusion, son," he continued. Colonel Forsett's Southern dialect seemed to be more pronounced when he was attempting to portray a fatherly image. He believed it helped put his men at ease, and he slipped into that drawl quite naturally.

Nothing could have shaken John more than if the colonel had told him that we had just nuked Hanoi. There must have been a mistake here. John was assured by the Navy recruiter that he would simply NOT be pulling a tour of duty in 'Nam.

"Not to question your last statement, sir, but are you sure that my orders are incorrect? I really was expecting to be at Subic for my overseas hitch and back in Pensacola for the remaining term of my enlistment." Not knowing just how the colonel would take his comment, John braced himself for a blast of indignation from him.

"Yeah, those recruiters are really something, aren't they?" he said and kind of chuckled. "Well, son, the reality is that you are here, and you will be here until you rotate back to the US."

To say that John's confidence in authority was being shaken to its core would have been an understatement. How could they get away with lying to someone just to get them to enlist and avoid the draft? It didn't seem fair—it wasn't fair. Damn him to hell, that son-of-a-bitch of a recruiter. John would be looking for him when, and if, he survived this tour of duty and rotated back to the world.

"Look, son," the colonel said. "You're probably thinking that this situation is not fair, right? Well, hell, Lieutenant, it isn't fair.

31

Nothing about Vietnam is fair. We are all here at the discretion of the people of the United States who elected the presidents who got us here and keep us here for whatever reasons they decide." And then with a calming tone in his voice, he said, "You have the character to make this thing work for you and your country. I personally picked you from a pool of officers and enlisted men for a mission that you will find as interesting as you find it difficult." Clearing his throat, he continued. "You see, John, we have a serious problem here in Saigon, and you have some particular tools that will help us find and solve these issues. I'm counting on you, son, to come through for God and country!"

And, with that, Colonel Forsett returned his gaze back to his desk, where he seemed to be deciphering topographical maps and communication logs with a deep, furrowed brow, reminding John of his Uncle Chad. Uncle Chad would get that look when he faced a legal case that had no clear cut solution and when he knew that continuing to labor over the problem would eventually wind up in a double shot of whiskey to calm his nerves. John admired his uncle because besides favoring him in appearance, their personalities were similar as well. Of course, Uncle Chad was a mover and a shaker. Everyone in the family knew that if Uncle Chad decided that something was going to happen, he would move heaven and Earth to make it so. He was a character that all the family admired and also worried about at the same time. A little unorthodox in his thinking, Uncle Chad was the kind of person whom everyone had an opinion of—good or bad, but an opinion nonetheless.

John could see that same dogged determination in Forsett that he both admired and disliked in his favorite uncle. He heard Forsett's words again in his mind, "You are here and you will be here until you rotate back to the US." That was it. Settled. No appeal. That son-of-a-bitch recruiter would wish he had never met John Bremen once he got through with him.

Grasping reality had never been a difficult thing for John, and this situation was about as real as anything had ever been in his life. He was here, and he would be here until his tour was up.

"So, what do I do now?" John mused to himself. What crossed his mind at that moment was Tuyen, some young Vietnamese women, and a fifth of Johnny Walker Black. Now was not the time for revenge...no, it was time for drinking!

Chapter 10

I need a drink!

John met with Klahan after the very unpleasant news from the colonel that shocked him into the reality that he was in a hot combat zone and would be for a minimum of twelve months, the normal tour of duty for a soldier in Vietnam. He was ready for a stiff drink and some frivolity with the local girls. Something in the back of his mind kept telling him that there was another factor involved that he just had not figured out that was influencing these recent events. He wasn't sure how, but he would figure it out one way or the other.

"So, John," Klahan queried. "How did it go with the new CO?"

"Not so well. It seems that this particular colonel has decided that I am the answer to his problems here in Saigon. Really a bummer, if you know what I mean. I planned to be soaking up some rays at Subic Bay on the tennis courts and spending lots of time in the Officer's Club." John's demeanor seemed to get graver as he recalled the perfect plan that he had had for himself before he had left the good old USA. This was definitely going to set those plans back, and he didn't like his current situation at all.

"We just never know what's in store for us from day to day, John," Klahan said, thinking back to his personal family tragedy and how it had changed his life forever. "I'm sure by the time this war is over and we have resumed our normal lives again that we will look back on these days as just routine events in an ever-changing scene."

"Quite the philosopher, aren't you, my friend?" John quipped. "What I need is a lot of scotch and a good timing Vietnamese sweetie to take my mind off of my troubles for a while. Do think that your lady friend Tuyen can hook us up with some young baby-sans? I'm ready to drink until I get drunk and screw until I pass out!"

"Don't worry, my friend," Klahan said to me with a wink and a friendly pat on the back. "We will make tonight your initiation into the world of Vietnamese night life! As long as you have the money, I will keep the booze and the baby-sans coming until you get your fill."

"Right now, money is the least of my worries. What else can you spend money on in this God-forsaken country?" If John was destined to be here for a miserably long year, he would make the most of his opportunity to sow some wild oats among the fields of Saigon.

Chapter 11

Klahan Goes Undercover

Klahan had just come from Colonel Forsett's office, and he was inspired! The colonel had shared some intelligence with him that could help him and Tuyen begin to track down the cowards who had killed their families in Hue. He couldn't wait to share the news with Tuyen, and when she came into the building that they had recently rented for their massage parlor, he began to tell her everything so fast that she had to stop him.

"Klahan, please slow down. I can't follow what you are trying to tell me," she said with a little giggle. "I haven't ever seen you so excited since I met you in Hue."

"Tuyen, I have much to tell you, and I think I have found an excellent way to continue to get information from the Americans about our families and their murderers," he said confidently. "I didn't want to tell you anything about my deal with the American colonel before I was sure that it would pay off for us, but now it appears that it will help us in so many ways to find and repay those who wronged us in Hue."

Tuyen looked at Klahan skeptically and asked, "What kind of deal did you make with the Americans?" She was worried that Klahan was getting in over his head and that she might be left alone in this huge city of Saigon.

"Don't worry, Little Angel," he said tenderly. "I will not do anything that will endanger your safety or happiness."

So he began to tell her about working for the colonel in an undercover capacity and that the colonel had promised to supply them with money, food and shelter if he would simply help the colonel catch the person leaking the information to the Viet Cong and the NVA troops.

"What he doesn't know," he laughed in a booming tone, "is that I would have helped him for free if he would only give us the information that we need. The way I see it now is that he needs us as much as we need him!" Klahan said seriously, "You know, Tuyen, I think it is time to put our massage parlor into play. How many other girls have you recruited to help us get information from the American and high-ranking ARVN soldiers?"

She thought for a few minutes and said, "Well, I have four girls willing to help us if we pay them and help them find their families. Do you think we can do that?"

"Oh, yes, Tuyen," he said confidently. I have a really good plan that will make all of our troubles go away."

"Thank you, Klahan, for taking good care of me and keeping me safe," Tuyen said with genuine sincerity. "I would not have made it to Saigon or have survived in this war torn place without your help."

"Don't you worry, Tuyen. We are on our way to victory." He smiled and gave her a big hug.

Chapter 12

Enticing LT Bremen to the Massage Parlor

Klahan reported to Colonel Forsett's office the next day, full of hope and optimism. For the first time since he and Tuyen had made their way from Hue to Saigon, they had a genuine opportunity to discover information that would expose the plot to kill their parents and family members. Klahan knew that by cooperating with the colonel, he would be able to discover much more information than he could do on his own.

"Let me tell you what I have in mind for you, Klahan," Forsett said. "I am going to confide in you because I believe that you will see that you and I have the same ultimate goal in mind for your country and for your beloved city of Hue. We need to influence Lieutenant John Bremen to help infiltrate the MACV staff to try and stem the tide of classified information being leaked to the enemy. Your friendship with him will make him more receptive to our ideas, and we need him to get on board with our plan as soon as possible."

Klahan nodded positively.

"What we need," the colonel went on, "is to integrate Bremen into the operation without him sensing that we have manipulated him to assist us in our task of finding the damaging information drain in the MACV Division." The colonel paused momentarily to give Klahan a chance to collect his thoughts before he went on.

"You see, Klahan, Bremen is a linguistic overachiever. He has mastered many languages, including Swahili, which you know is one of the ways that 'Charlie' communicates with its base in North Vietnam. If we can place Bremen in a strategic place with his true purpose unknown to anyone but you, Briggs, and me, we will have an excellent chance to discover who the traitor in my outfit is."

"So, how can I help, Colonel?"

"Well, first of all, you need to keep him feeling good about your friendship and continue to gain his confidence on a daily basis. Once we have convinced him of the inevitability of his expertise in our operation, we can come clean and let him know how and why he was recruited."

"Do you really think that's a good approach, sir, letting him know that we tricked him into being transferred to Vietnam? Aren't you afraid that he will blow up and want to expose what we are doing to Washington?"

"Once we have taken him into our confidence and let him know the lengths that we have gone to secure his help, he will be more than willing to come around. But first and foremost, we must compromise him where he won't really have a choice if he does change his mind about helping us."

"Take him out, get him knee-walking drunk and continue to win him over to you personally. Once we have built that personal bond between us, he will not compromise any of us in the future."

"I'll do that, sir. You can count on me to get it done quickly," he said as the colonel was packing up his briefcase and heading toward the door to his office.

*   *   *   *   *

Klahan had so much on his mind that when he first saw John at the sidewalk bar drinking Ba-Moui-Ba, the Vietnamese beer that was referred to as "Tiger Piss" by the American soldiers, he almost didn't recognize him. This local concoction—which may or may not have contained formaldehyde—could get you high, and John tried it, although he had promised himself that he would only drink things off base in Saigon that were pressurized. However, at this particular juncture in his short Vietnamese tour of duty, all of his inhibitions had flown out the window.

"John," called Klahan. "Are you drunk yet?" he mused as he sat down. "You look like crap, my friend," Klahan said and ordered a Ba-Moui-Ba for himself.

"Well, if I'm not drunk yet, I will be soon," John said and took another slug of this local legendary drink of the masses. "Actually, after the first couple of these beers, I couldn't taste anything anyway," John quipped as he slid his glass back to the bar maid to refill. "To say that this has been a shitty day, week and month would be an understatement on a grand scale."

Klahan said cheerfully, "Well, tonight is your lucky night, my friend! Tonight you will be lying in the arms of a beautiful baby-san that will make you forget all of your troubles. I actually have opened a massage parlor with the girl Tuyen that I had mentioned to you before, and she has some of the prettiest baby-sans in all of Saigon!" he boasted. "I think it's time to visit her and get your attitude adjusted," he said as he helped John to his feet.

Klahan got John and all of his things into a rented Lambretta, and they were off to the Magic Fingers Steam and Cream Massage Parlor. John would be happy there, at least for the time being, and Tuyen and her girls would help John forget his problems for the immediate future.

*   *   *   *   *

The Magic Fingers Steam and Cream Massage Parlor was pretty much what the name described. These massage parlors were operated in full view of everyone in Saigon, and although prostitution was officially illegal in Saigon, the authorities would turn their heads and permit such activities to happen if certain conditions were met. First of all, money was paid to the Saigon government for special permission to operate such an establishment; second, there were to be no public acts of sexual contact visible from the street; and finally, there was to be no violence that would attract attention to the activity going on in the massage parlor.

The Magic Fingers Steam and Cream Massage Parlor was a high end facility, catering mostly to American GIs and ARVN officials. It boasted a well-mannered and beautiful host of geisha girls, and Klahan had hired some off-duty Korean soldiers as bouncers. No one wanted to get tangled up with these dudes. First of all, they were big and looked mean as hell. They spoke very little but would literally throw you out on your ass if you so much as questioned Tuyen and the other girls about their prices and practices. The bouncers gave a new meaning to the word mercenaries.

Klahan had told Tuyen earlier in the day of his plan to bring John by, and he wanted to make sure she understood that she and her girls were to make John so comfortable that he would have no desire to leave and stay anywhere else. The colonel had told Klahan that he would instruct John in the morning that he was to be dressed in civilian clothes and live among the local population for the particular job that he had in mind for him. John had shared that info with Klahan on the way over to the Steam and Cream, so it was natural to assume that his new friend in Saigon would put him up until he could find more suitable accommodations. A warm welcome greeted John when he and Klahan arrived at the parlor.

"Welcome to our little slice of heaven," Tuyen said to John when he and Klahan walked from the Lambretta to the parlor. "We understand that you may be staying with us for a while, and we want to make you feel very warm and comfortable here."

As Tuyen was saying this, she had two of her prettiest geisha girls come up to John and begin helping him to a room in the back of the building, where he could get undressed and comfortable. He was already pretty soused with the Tiger Beer, and his resistance, had there been any from the outset, was non-existent at this point. After a few minutes, Tuyen and Klahan heard the girls running a bath for John and giggling, as they were obviously giving him a bath and entertaining him in true geisha-girl style.

41

"Klahan," Tuyen began with a look of concern, "does the colonel know that we are housing John Bremen here at the Steam and Cream, and would he approve?"

Klahan thought for a moment and said with confidence, "I think the colonel will be most happy and satisfied that we have taken John under our wing and made it easy for him to disappear into the civilian area of Saigon. He told me to win John's confidence. That is what we are doing!"

"OK, Klahan. I have nowhere else to put my trust but in you. We will make John so happy that he will not even think of going anywhere else to stay," she said with a smile and left Klahan with his thoughts of meeting the next day with the colonel.

Chapter 13

Klahan Takes John to Forsett's Office

Klahan was in Colonel Forsett's office at 8:00 AM the next morning to get his next set of instructions for LT Bremen. The colonel seemed to be in a pleasant mood, and Klahan was happy to speak to him about continuing to build their alliance with the purpose of detecting and destroying those responsible for his current status in Saigon.

"Did you keep LT Bremen in good spirits and out of trouble last night, Klahan?" the colonel asked him when he entered the office from the front door sidewalk.

"Yes, sir," Klahan replied with optimism.

"Good, good," the colonel replied and opened a folder on his desk and began to look through it carefully before he spoke again. "I have been giving this a lot of thought, and I think I have figured out how we need to play this situation to get the maximum effect of John's addition to our counter surveillance team. We need to isolate him from the other officers in the command, and we need to introduce him as a private contractor for MACV who is working on special orders from Washington," he said, finishing his thought. "I think if we make it appear that John is here for a different reason other than helping us find the security breach, then he will have a pretty good chance of figuring out how to fix the problem quietly and under the radar."

Klahan looked dubious, so Forsett assured him, "Look, we will have him come to my office tomorrow. I want you here with me so we can clear the air and get John fully on board with this project. This could be a dangerous mission, and he will need to volunteer before I can put him in the position he needs to be in to make a difference. We need to get this all out in the open, so

John won't find out about this accidentally. Let's make it ten hundred hours."

Klahan agreed and had one more question to ask of the colonel before he left his office. "Colonel, have you found any more information about the Battle for Hue and any details that I can use to pursue the monsters that killed my family?"

"Not yet," the colonel replied, "but I am working on it for you and your sister. I will see you tomorrow."

Klahan pulled Tuyen aside when he returned to the massage parlor and explained what the colonel had confided in him and cautioned her not to speak of any of it to John Bremen.

"Oh," she laughed out loud, "John Bremen is so relaxed right now that he is not worried about much of anything, and especially not about war things. He's been sipping single malt scotch whiskey all afternoon and rolling in the covers with three of our prettiest girls. He's in a proper state of mind," Tuyen said with a smile, "that will last until morning."

What Klahan had to do was make sure John made it on time to the colonel's office, so he could finally share with him all of the twists and turns that had already taken place in this plan. He was sure he could get that done.

Chapter 14

Introducing Bill Hicks

It was a typical summer day in Saigon, and the afternoon monsoon rain was on the horizon. The temperature was in the lower nineties, with the humidity around 90% -- not the kind of day to be in a non-air conditioned office. Since this was a meeting of the highest order of security, each participant was dressed in his best uniform, and they all looked like as though they were dedicated to getting down to business.

Colonel Forsett had left word for John to report to his office the next day at ten hundred hours in civilian clothes. John was a good officer, and he never questioned orders, that is, unless they made no sense to him at all. When that did happen, like when he was sent to Saigon for a two-week TDY mission, he would inquire of the senior officer in a respectful and disciplined way. However, there was never a question in his mind as to whether he would follow the orders that he was given. It just wasn't in his DNA to disobey or ignore an order from a superior officer. So, he was in khakis and a flowered Hawaiian shirt when he reported to the colonel's office. He did think that it was unusual that Klahan was going to be in the meeting with the CO as well. However, John was too good of a sailor to try to make too much logic from a coincidental situation.

Colonel Forsett, Briggs, Klahan, John Bremen, and someone whom John had never met before were all sitting around the colonel's desk, and although John had not personally met SGT Major Briggs before, it was common knowledge who the man was and what he represented. The other man in the room in civilian clothes was a bit more interesting. What made the encounter with the man so unique was that while he spoke to the colonel and the other people in the room in English, he spoke to John in

Swahili. That was odd enough, but when he did speak to John in Swahili, no one seemed to notice or care. Now THAT was weird, John thought to himself.

So who was this mystery man in civvies who seemed to know everyone but John? There was one way to find out for sure, John thought to himself, and he was about to launch out on that quest when the colonel chimed into the conversation.

"John, I know you probably have some questions about this meeting and just exactly what it means," the colonel said. "Of course, you know Klahan, and you've no doubt heard of SGT Major Briggs. Let me introduce you to Harry Jones. Harry is a contractor for us here at MACV, and he takes care of certain chores that we occasionally need handling that are a little sensitive and that don't need to be run through Command operations."

After this introduction, Harry rose to his feet and with a big smile stuck out his hand and welcomed John into the special operations unit that he was about to learn more about than he cared to know.

"Harry," Forsett began, "why don't you tell John a little about what you do for us and how you feel he can assist us in our special operations unit?"

Without any hesitation, Harry said, "I will do that, J.P."

John almost fell out of his chair! Who the hell refers to a 0-6 level officer by his initials, and why did the colonel not look surprised at Harry's response? This was going to get interesting for sure.

"John," Harry began, "as the colonel said a few minutes ago, there are some sensitive issues that are best handled away from this command and more independently than would normally be the case in a combat zone. There are some unique problems within the MACV command that we need to address that may have serious implications back home if we are not successful in our approach to controlling them here. As the colonel may have informed you when you were first assigned to this unit, there appears to be an informant leaking unauthorized material that is ultimately getting into the hands of the enemy. What makes things worse, this appears to be more than an ordinary scheme to sell information to the enemy for money, drugs, or other items of value to the individual creating the problem."

"The CIA has credible information that along with the information leak, there appears to be some type of information for weapons deals going on to boot. We have been getting close to the source of the leak, but we have not zeroed in on the person causing us so much damage. That's where you come into the picture." He paused and looked at the other men in the room before continuing his story.

"You may have some questions as to why you are in civilian clothes and why you have not been billeted in the BOQ on base. Let me address that question this way." He continued without hesitation. "As far as everyone in this room is concerned, you are who you are – Lieutenant John Bremen, a naval officer with linguistic abilities that far exceed the normal demands of an assignment in Southeast Asia. However, from this day forward you will cease to be John Bremen and will become Bill Hicks, a private contractor working with the GAO and on TDY here in Saigon. You will have special authority to go anywhere necessary to ensure that the safety of any operational task is in compliance with the US Government safety standards issued by the GAO." He paused to take a drink of coffee.

The GAO, or Government Accounting Office, was the ultimate authority used for auditing, evaluating, and investigating services performed on behalf of the US Government. When the GAO determined that something was amiss, it could begin an investigation that could eventually shut down any operation without having to get approval by the Joint Chiefs or anyone else in the government. The GAO worked as the watchdog for the US Congress and was the people's eyes and ears on how government spending was being carried out. So, the simple presence of such an individual on assignment to Saigon was a continual threat to all commanders at all levels of command. This would be John's cover.

John had been trying to take all of this information into his head and follow the logic, but the presence of Klahan and SGT Briggs in the room further confused John. How did they figure into this complicated scene? Although he wanted to ask some questions for clarification, he thought it better to wait until he was asked if he had questions about his new assignment.

"So, John, let's give you a little profile, your background, and some personal data that will make your stay here more believable. Bill Hicks grew up in Birmingham, Alabama. He went to college at Ashburn University and applied for a job with the government because he was classified 4F, a result of his flat feet, and could not join the military to serve his country as an active military person. Bill's sense of pride and the need to serve his country in some capacity during this time of unrest caused him to apply for a job with the US Government Accounting Office, and the rest is history. Do you have any questions to this point?"

"To say I didn't have any questions would be a lie, but I think I would rather hear the whole story before I trouble you with my thoughts and questions," John replied.

Harry explained to John why such an operation was needed and how not finding the leak could impact the US mainland forever. It had been reported by the FBI that multiple cases of AK-47 Chinese Communist rifles had been showing up in San Francisco. These automatic rifles had been dispersed throughout some of the crime families across the US. There was a cooperative effort between the CIA and the FBI, and it appeared that there was some sort of connection between these illegal firearms and the information leak that was emanating from somewhere in the MACV Headquarters operation.

"Your job will be to help us surveil everyone in the MACV operation. Everyone, and I mean everyone, is a suspect, with the exception of the people in this room. Generals to corporals, admirals to petty officers, airmen, and even civilian employees working for the US Government are all fair game. We will leave no stone unturned until we find this S.O.B. and eliminate the threat," Harry said, sitting back down in his chair across from the colonel.

The colonel had been watching John during this entire illumination of the mission's goals, and he thought that John was buying into this plan quite well. Colonel Forsett turned to John. "So, John, what questions do you have for us? Surely you have some, right?"

"Sir, how does Klahan fit into all of this? He is a Vietnamese national civilian, and I don't understand where he comes into play in this plan."

The colonel smiled and said, "John, I need to make something clear to you at this point.   You have to volunteer for this assignment for it to go forward. This is a dangerous mission that could get you captured, tortured or killed. I will not force you to play ball with us, but if you are willing to take on the mantle of responsibility for helping your country, find these traitors and merchants of death, I will give you all the other details concerning the mission. If you decide that it is too dangerous for you or that you cannot commit 100% to this mission, then I will personally see that your orders are amended and that you are sent back to your posh assignment in Subic Bay. The choice is yours, but I need to know now if this is something that you are willing to commit to until the job is completed successfully. I'll give you a few minutes to consider the implications, John, and then we will go with your decision as to how we move forward with this mission."

The colonel picked up his coffee mug and took a slug of the cold coffee.

"I do have a couple of questions, sir, if that's not a problem."

"Not at all, son," the colonel answered.

"Klahan," the colonel said, addressing the young Vietnamese man sitting to the left of John, "would you like to fill John in on how you fit into the mission?" The colonel knew that this was a point of no return for the mission. John could become enraged

49

once he found out that he had been manipulated into this position and that it wasn't just a directive of the War Department. Forsett was betting on John's character and fortitude to help him make the decision to do the right thing.

"Yes, sir." Klahan looked at the colonel and then back to his new friend, John Bremen. Klahan started at the beginning of his story of how he and Tuyen had been orphaned by the V.C. and the NVA armies when they overran Hue and killed their families. Without pausing to gather his thoughts, Klahan spoke firmly and with purpose as to his and Tuyen's plan to find the murderous cowards and bring an end to their reign of terror.

"John, I met SGT Major Briggs and became his personal driver once I got settled in Saigon. We gained mutual respect for each other, and through my contact with SGT Major Briggs, I was fortunate to meet Colonel Forsett. He asked me if I were willing and able to commit to seeking true revenge on those who had devastated my family, and I told him 'yes' and began to work with him and SGT Major Briggs to find out who killed my family."

At this point, Klahan paused and looked at both Briggs and Forsett and then continued his story. "The colonel asked me if I would arrange to bump into you casually in Bangkok while you were on leave, and we devised a plan that would help us decide if you were the right man for this mission. I guess you have figured it out by now, but you not only passed the test; you have more qualifications than we actually need to make this thing happen. I didn't accidentally run into you in Saigon on your first day in Vietnam. We planned the encounter to make sure it happened, but in such a manner that it would seem like incidental contact. This has all been planned and charted to get you to this moment and this decision today. I have committed my life to this mission. I will redeem my family's honor and execute judgement on those who have brought all of this pain into my life. I had to make that decision on my own, and so you will have to decide if your very life is worth ending some of the misery that this war is causing both here and in America."

Klahan dropped his head as if in silent prayer to his ancestors for their approval of his goal of avenging their deaths.

Everything now fell into place for John. He realized he would need to sharpen his observation skills even more in the weeks and months to come to stay alive. After hearing Klahan's personal story of loss and sacrifice, John could hardly turn a deaf ear on a mission that had a purpose to improve the greater good in both Vietnam and the US.

"Colonel," John said with a renewed vigor that surprised even himself, "I'm in. What do you need for me to do?"

Chapter 15

Developing a Plan

The colonel dismissed everyone, with the exception of Klahan and John Bremen. Now they we going to get down to the details on how they would pull off this surveillance mission and catch a thief and traitorous coward.

The colonel began describing some facets of the mission that made perfect sense, even if they were somewhat unorthodox in their origin. John was to immediately assume the role and personal characteristics of Bill Hicks, GAO worker extraordinaire. The colonel wanted John to actually live the part of Bill Hicks, not just simulate this Bill Hicks persona when dealing with people who had not yet been cleared of this conspiracy.

"John," the colonel spoke in an almost rehearsed tone, "you will no longer refer to me as 'Sir' or 'Colonel,' but rather as Harry refers to me--as J.P.—when we speak in public. We will need to come up with procedures to pass information back and forth in a secure method to avoid our plan leaking out to the overall staff. I'll think on that and get back with you as soon as I have figured out the most secure way to get that done."

"Klahan, this is where your massage parlor and Tuyen's girls can help. If our traitor is using the services of an establishment like the Steam and Cream Massage Parlor, then we should be able to track him through his visits in the city of Saigon. We both know that the only thing the operators of these flop houses like more than money is to spread gossip about their competitors' places. We can put that knowledge to good use to try and flush out this guy. Do you think Tuyen will play along with us on this?"

"After all you have done for both Tuyen and me, I can assure you we will do whatever we can to help you find your bad guy," Klahan replied, expressing genuine thankfulness for the colonel's financial and political support that had enabled them to open and operate their massage parlor.

"I will speak to her today when I leave here. Do you have a plan, sir, to flush this guy out, or should we just keep our eyes and ears open for information about thefts of weapons and payments for illegal contraband?"

"The first thing that we need to do is to give John an opportunity to go through the duty roster of all senior personnel who would have had access to the intelligence documents that have been leaked," the colonel said. "Once we have narrowed down our subjects, we will want to flush them out so we can trace the flow of intelligence and determine who and why they are doing this. Everyone who works in areas of such top secret information is screened for their security clearances, so we will not be starting from scratch. We will have some data to analyze that should help us narrow the field quite quickly. John's ability to eavesdrop on these suspects as a general contractor for the GAO should also help us move with dispatch to sew this thing up in a timely manner. The longer we take to determine how all of this intelligence data and weapons smuggling fits together, the more danger is going to be imposed upon the US mainland. We need for this to happen quickly, Klahan, or our homeland could resemble Vietnam in the violence and instability that such a weapon could inflict upon everyday people in the US."

Klahan held his hand out to the colonel and shook it vigorously. He shook John's hand as well.

"Gentlemen," Klahan stated with the confidence of a prize fighter, "I'm ready."

Chapter 16

Bill Hicks Meets Tuyen and Her Girls

When Klahan arrived back at the Steam and Cream, he took Tuyen aside and went over everything that had transpired with the colonel just hours before. He said to her with commitment, "Tuyen, we must do this for Colonel Forsett. He has been like a father to us these past few months. We owe him our very lives for financially and politically sponsoring us and getting us off the street. We are now in a safe, secure place of business, and we have a home for the first time since we lost our families in Hue. None of that would have happened without the colonel's help and blessing."

"My girls and I will do whatever is necessary to help this great man," Tuyen said to Klahan, taking his hand and squeezing it firmly. "Just tell us what you want us to do, and I will make sure it happens. These young women will do as I ask, and their loyalty to me and to you is unlimited."

"That is wonderful, Tuyen," he said. "As soon as the colonel gives me the details of the overall plan, we will decide the best way to supply the information and support to him. John Bremen is part of the plan, and we will begin referring to him as Bill Hicks going forward. His cover story is that he is an employee of the US General Accounting Office and that he is in Saigon to inspect the procurement and safety issues for the American forces in this city and in all of South Vietnam. We must make sure that all of your girls know him only as Bill Hicks, and not John Bremen. Only you and I will know who he really is and what his real mission is here in Saigon. He will be infiltrating the MACV operation, trying to find out who is leaking confidential and top secret information to the Viet Cong and the NVA. You must promise me that you will not share that information with anyone other than me. Don't even let John know that you know the truth about his personal situation or his mission. Can you do that for me?"

"Of course," she said. "I have already forgotten everything about him that we learned yesterday." She smiled and went into the main room with all of the other geisha girls.

When John came home and knocked on the front door of the Steam and Cream parlor, Tuyen opened the door and greeted him with a smile.

"Bill Hicks, I believe that we have made accommodations for your stay here in Saigon," Tuyen said as she ushered him into the establishment and into a nice bedroom that she had prepared for him. "A couple of our girls will visit you after dinner and help you relax from your hard day of work. Dinner will be at 6:00 PM downstairs in the great hall near the rear of the building."

Dinner was a traditional meal featuring rice and fish and local rice wine. The cuisine was unusual for John, but it was tasty, and the last thing he was going to do was ask what he was eating and how it was prepared. He just ate his fill, drank too much wine, and excused himself to his bedroom.

As John was getting settled in his room, two lovely young Vietnamese girls came in and began helping him unpack his things. One of them went into the bathroom and began drawing a bath for him. When he had finished putting everything away, he turned to thank the girls and found them both naked and standing before the tub in a welcoming fashion. These were beautiful young women, both with small, firm breasts, narrow waists, and slightly rounded hips. They did not appear to be embarrassed being naked before him, and one of them came up to him and began helping him take off his clothes. He could already tell from the bulge in his shorts that arousal was not going to be a problem with these two beauties. Before he knew it, he was naked and standing before these angelic young women, one of whom proceeded to rub and caress his cock and balls. As he was about to explode, she stopped massaging him, invited him into the bath, and both girls began to soap him up and bathe him as if he were a king. It didn't take long for him to reach an unbelievable climax with these two young women, and he thought to himself that this was going to be a great tour of duty in Saigon! These girls helped him out of the bath, dried him off thoroughly, gave him a silk bathrobe to wear and repeated the sexual experience that had so electrified him in the tub. He was truly spent by the time they left him around 11:00 PM. He dressed in a pair of boxer shorts and tee shirt and climbed into bed. He was asleep before his head hit the pillow.

The next morning, John was awakened by these same two young women. They had prepared a nice breakfast of rice cereal and coffee, and they asked him if there was anything else that he needed.

"No," John said, thinking of how nice the evening experience had been. As John transported himself mentally back to the previous evening, Tuyen came into the room.

"Mr. Bill Hicks," she started, "Klahan and I have decided to ask you to be our guest here at our home and business as long as you are in Saigon. I hope you will find your stay a pleasant one."

John thought to himself, "If it were more pleasant, I would have to die and go to heaven!" Then he laughed at his simple thoughts of future pleasures at the Magic Fingers Steam and Cream Massage Parlor and began to get ready for his next meeting with the colonel.

Chapter 17

Bill Hicks of the GAO

John stopped by the colonel's office for a short briefing and then began to prepare for his first day of work as a trusted and somewhat feared member of the office of the GAO. The first thing John had to do was compile a list of all of the people who had access to the classified information that had been leaked and isolate those on the list for further research into their backgrounds. Next, he had the colonel's office contact the S-2 office in Washington to have the background files on each of those potential suspects sent to him so he could determine who, if anyone, had a motive for those thefts. It would take about a week to get the information to him by secure courier, and in the meantime John would make it his mission to meet each of these people and begin to analyze them so he could put everything together once the files had been delivered. In all, there were twenty-seven potential people who had access to the files in question. The difficult part of this entire mission was to determine who had been reading the files and sharing them outside of the MACV operation.

The key to this dilemma was motive. There had to be some very strong motive for anyone to put himself into such a position of compromise, knowing that if he were eventually caught that he could be tried for treason. He was trying not to form any opinions about anyone until he had all of the facts of the case and had analyzed them thoroughly.

While he was waiting on the personnel files from Washington, he could do a little snooping around to see if there were any red flags that might alert him to irregular activity with anyone. He had narrowed the list of possible suspects to twenty-seven people initially; then, he had eliminated another twenty people due to their proximity and the difficulty they would have copying the data and smuggling it out of the secure area where they worked. The guards were very thorough when someone entered or exited the S-2 section of the MACV compound. John could see that about the only way one could smuggle things out of that office was through a body cavity, and he really doubted that was happening on a routine basis.

That left seven people who had access to the classified material in question. Those people were--Colonel Forsett; Briggs; Klahan; Captain Lawrence Baker, the security officer; Corporal Danny Banks, the Morning Report Clerk; Major Gerald Beckers, the communications officer; and PFC Jonathan Springs, who signed everyone into and out of the secure office space. He knew he could rule out Forsett, Briggs, and Klahan because they were part of the plan to catch and fix the leak. That left Baker, Banks, Gerald Beckers, and Jonathan Springs. He decided to concentrate on these four individuals because the odds were that one of them was involved in the theft of the classified material.

John looked at each man's personal data that was available at the MACV office there in Saigon. Each man's file jacket was complete as far as his name, rank, serial number, duty assignment, and details that were pertinent to his actual job description. However, there was no background profile on any of them. He would just have to wait until the files arrived in Saigon to get any more details about each person. If he dug too deeply at this point, he could lose his cover and foul up the entire plan. He kept telling himself over and over, "Be patient, John. Be patient!"

While John was waiting for his files to come from Washington, Klahan was doing a little surveillance work himself. He had asked John if he had made any progress on the possible suspects in the S-2 office, and John filled him in on the details that he knew about each man in question. Klahan had been given a special pass by Briggs, so he could come and go as needed to deliver Briggs to whatever location he needed to be driven. This was helpful to get

Klahan close to a couple of the people in question without raising questions in the minds of those two guys. Corporal Banks and PFC Springs were more accessible to Klahan because they ate at the base mess hall and carried on a pretty much normal life for enlisted men in the Saigon area. Also, both of them were pretty low in rank, so they were limited in their ability to frequent the high end massage parlors in Saigon. Through her contacts, Tuyen had told Klahan that Banks had no history with any of the brothels or massage parlors in Saigon. Tuyen had been talking with the other massage parlors in Saigon, and none of them had been visited by Banks. On the other hand, PFC Springs was a regular at Top of the Moon Massage Parlor down in the Cholon District of Saigon. Tuyen told Klahan that she would pay the girls in Cholon to see what they could find out about Springs and what he did on a daily basis in the S-2 office.

"I will get them to slip him some of their heroin to loosen him up and get him talking. Between that and their sexual techniques, we will find out if he is the one who is the thief in the office," she said confidently. "If we find out something like that, what should we do?"

"You do nothing. You simply let me know what he says and don't repeat it to anyone but me. We don't want to spook him if he is the leak, and we will want to find out who he is working with as well," Klahan said. "I'm sure the colonel will want whoever is causing all of these problems watched until we find his source of funding and the destination of the information that he is stealing."

With that, Tuyen told Klahan that she would know more about PFC Springs in a day or two and report back.

Chapter 18

An Untimely Visit from a Senator

It took about five days to get the files from Washington, but they were finally delivered to Colonel Forsett's office, and he immediately left a message for John that the files were indeed there.

"So, J.P.," John asked the colonel on the phone, "you got the package from home that you were expecting?"

"That's right, Bill. You should come by and enjoy some of these treats from home!" the colonel continued. "They were cooked up with you in mind," Forsett said, using the coded phrase that they had agreed on.

"I'll be right over. I sure don't want to miss out on good stuff from home," John said with a laugh.

When John entered the colonel's office, there was someone present that he did not know. This visitor was, however, a very powerful man back in the world. A big man with a loud voice, he was blustering quite a bit when John entered the office. He would soon find out that Senator Carlos Carlson, the senior senator from Maryland, was in Saigon "on a fact finding mission." Carlson was on the powerful US Committee on Foreign Relations, and no one wanted to rock the boat when this man was in town.

"Senator Carlson," the colonel began firmly, "let me introduce you to Bill Hicks, one of the GAO inspectors from Washington. He is here to evaluate the overall performance of our MACV operations, and I'm sure he will be happy to answer any questions you may have in the area of his expertise."

"Well, son," the senator began, "just how have you found things here in Saigon pertaining to the efficiency of the operation?"

"Senator, I have found a few things that need to be addressed, but I am just getting started, so you will have to bear with me a while until I get finished with my complete inspection. I can't imagine that there are too many things out of order, or we would have been sent over sooner," he said with a little smile on his face.

"Well, Bill, I just landed a short time ago, and I thought that I would surprise the colonel with my visit at MACV Headquarters. I do believe I accomplished that goal!" Carlson winked at the colonel to let him know that this old senator was a mover and a shaker. He would not simply sit in his office in D.C. and take a field commander's words for anything. No, he would see for himself.

"Bill," the colonel addressed John with a far off look of resolution, "could you give the senator and me a few minutes? I think we are just finishing up our conversation. Wouldn't you agree, Senator?"

"Well, I'm sure we will have another opportunity to speak before I leave for D.C. later in the week," the senator said, nodding. "The next time, I will show you the courtesy of giving you a call first before I just appear," the senator reassured him. Senator Carlson rose from his chair, said goodbye, and left Forsett's office.

Once the colonel and John were alone in the office, the colonel exploded in a rage. "That son-of-a-bitch knows better than to just show up in my office with no advance notice. A first-year law student knows that. What the hell does he think he is doing?" the colonel began to almost yell at no one in particular. Having realized that he was losing control, Colonel Forsett began to lower his voice to its natural speaking level, and he changed the subject immediately.

"I'm beginning to believe that this security lapse and the subsequent arms smuggling into the US is much more than what it seemed initially," Forsett told John. "Now I ask you, why would a senior senator who is very active on the Foreign Relations

Committee in the Senate fly 9,000+ miles to pop in on a colonel in the MACV operations division? I'll tell you what I think." The colonel's voice began to rise in volume and heat up again. "There's something that stinks about this whole damn thing," he concluded as he handed the files over to John. "Let's get right on these files and see if your findings implicate anyone in the S-2 office."

"Yes, sir," John said, using the normal protocol to speak to a superior officer. He would not abuse the opportunity to speak to the colonel in a familiar tone, and he would only do so when the ruse of his being a civilian was in play.

"Klahan and I have been working somewhat behind the scene to find out as much as possible in regards to the four people who, we think, could have connections to the theft of the documents and espionage that is continuing to take place in this division. I am hoping that these files will shed some light on all of them and get us closer to determining which one is the traitor. I plan to visit with Klahan and see if he has discovered more personal information on our suspects. Between what is in these files and what he has discovered, I am hoping to be able to give you a name soon, sir," John concluded with the colonel. "Excellent, LT Bremen. I knew I could count on you and your ability to help us solve this dilemma."

Chapter 19

The Four Suspects Identified

John sat down with the files that he had acquired from the colonel and began to disseminate the data, cross referencing what he already knew about each of the four potential security leaks that these represented. Corporal Banks was the first person that John researched, and John thought he was clearly not a suspect after just a few minutes of reading his security file. He was born in Atlanta, Georgia, and he appeared to be an All American boy. There was absolutely nothing in his file that would indicate that he was even capable of committing a treasonous act, much less prone to do so. John was able to dismiss any thought of Banks being involved in anything illegal or immoral.

The next candidate for John's scrutiny was PFC Springs. Springs was from Arkansas, and his early life experiences consisted of working on a farm outside of Texarkana, Arkansas. He finished high school ranked somewhere just below the average student in his class, had left town for a while to work on some oil rigs in Midland/Odessa, and came back home a year or so later after getting into some trouble with the local authorities over a couple of DUI charges and resisting arrest in one of the local bars in the Midland area. The agreement that the authorities had made with Springs was that if he would leave the Midland/Odessa area, all charges of his arrest and potential incarceration would be expunged. He was a country boy, but he wasn't a dumb country boy, so he left Midland/Odessa abruptly and returned home to the farm. Of course, you can never go home again and have everything be the same, so he didn't fit in there anymore either. So, he did the smart thing that country boys from Arkansas did back in 1966, and he joined the Army. With the exception of some wild partying and a couple of accusations of womanizing from nearby neighbors, he really didn't have any suspicious background issues that indicated a red flag for John. He wasn't married and had no family, other than his mom and dad back on the farm. John eliminated Springs from his list of suspects as well.

That left MAJ Gerald Beckers and CPT Baker. Baker was the security officer for that particular secure office area, and Gerald Beckers was the communications officer for the same office. Either of these guys would have had unlimited access and control of these files that were leaked to the outside world. Now it was up to John and Klahan's crew to find out which one was the culprit.

John took the remaining files out of his briefcase and spread them on the table in front of him. The first one he chose to review was Gerald Beckers. Beckers was a West Point Graduate and was on a career track to make general before he retired if he kept his nose clean and continued to excel in the positions that he was put into by MACV operations. He had been in country for two tours of duty, back to back, and it was somewhat unusual for that to happen for communication officers at MACV. John made a notation of that fact and continued to move through his classified personnel jacket methodically. About the time he was just settling down into a steady pace of reviewing Beckers' file, Klahan came into the office and sat down with him at the table.

"So, John," he said. "Did you find anything unusual from any of our four potential suspects?"

"I went through PFC Springs and Corporal Banks' folders and pretty much eliminated them as suspects. Were Tuyen and her girls able to find out anything about those two from her contacts with the massage parlors in Saigon?" he asked. "The corporal is as clean as a whistle. He probably hasn't ever even spit on the sidewalk," John laughed. "Did you find anything on him with your research from Tuyen?"

"Not on Banks," Klahan said, "but our boy Springs is a bit more interesting. He regularly visited some of the lower class massage parlors down in Cholon. To be precise, the Top of the Moon

Massage Parlor in Cholon says that PFC Springs is a regular customer of theirs, and they reported that he was both physically abusive and just downright mean when he spent time with their girls," he continued. "According to what they told Tuyen, he would probably be arrested if he tried some of that stuff in the States."

"Did they say if he bragged to any of the girls about his job or what he did for the MACV operation?" John asked.

"No, but I would say he's probably not your spy or even involved in the mishandling of the secret material in question. He doesn't appear to be a very bright dude—just a nasty, mean little punk who beats up on women and those less able to defend themselves," Klahan said.

"I've been through his classified personnel jacket as well, and I tend to agree with you. He seems a little too simple to pull off something as complex as the theft of classified material right under the noses of all of the security personnel and then somehow turn that into an exchange for AK-47 rifles," John said. "I guess I am left with the two officers in the security office to investigate. They may prove to be a little more difficult to eliminate them as suspects."

"I am going to see Tuyen this afternoon, and she has been checking on our two officers in question. I will get that information to you, assuming there is some information to share, as soon as possible," Klahan said and left the office.

Chapter 20

Looks Can be Deceiving

When Klahan went home, he called Tuyen and took her inside an interior room in the massage parlor to speak with her privately.

"So, have you found out anything about the two officers and if they have used any massage parlors in the Saigon area? Both of these officers hold higher military rank than the enlisted men and probably have more disposable income, so it might be easier for them to spend some of their money on geisha girls," Klahan said.

"Funny you should mention that," she said with a satisfied grin. "I have located two massage parlors where CPT Baker spent quite a lot of time and money. I have the name of the madam, and you might want to visit her in person, as she wasn't willing to talk to me over the telephone. One of the parlors is in Cholon, and it is the same one that the PFC had been going to. Do you think there is a connection? The major that you asked me about doesn't seem to have ever visited any massage parlor in Saigon, so I guess he's a nice guy and in the clear, too."

"Great, I'll share this info with John. It looks like we might have found our security leak," Klahan sighed with relief.

Klahan immediately jumped into his jeep and drove over to the colonel's office, where John was working with the files of the two officers in question.

"John, we may have found the guy who has been leaking the info. I won't know until I talk to the madam at Top of the Moon Massage Parlor over in Cholon. Would you believe that it is the same one that our PFC Springs has been going to as well? Do you think that is a coincidence? What are the odds that they just happen to be getting laid at the same brothel?" Klahan asked.

John had been reading the other files that he had received from the colonel on Baker and Beckers. He surprised Klahan when he said, "I too have been busy, Klahan. I have studied these two files on the officers, and they just don't add up to me. On the one hand, CPT Baker appears to be the loose cannon with questionable connections to the social underground in Saigon. He's a whoremonger and really not a very nice guy, to say the least. However, he's only been in country for a few months, and I don't see how he could have already set up a network of arms for information deal with the enemy. On the other hand, MAJ Beckers has been here for over one and one-half years. That would give him lots of time to begin networking with someone outside the American jurisdiction and provide him a way to move the documents."

Klahan thought for a moment and then said, "Beckers looks like a boy scout on paper. Whatever could drive him to doing something as stupid as leaking classified info, and for what reason?"

John opened the folders and showed Klahan what he had discovered about the two officers. Baker had grown up in a lower middle-class neighborhood in Detroit, attended a small mid-western college and entered the ROTC program. When he graduated, he was commissioned a 2nd Lieutenant in the US Army. He was originally assigned to a supply depot, Defense Depot Ogden, where he had served for two and a half years. In that time, he was promoted to 1st Lieutenant and he reenlisted before his tour of duty expired with the promise of a promotion to Captain, assuming his performance evaluations were positive. Once promoted to Captain, he was reassigned to the MACV in Saigon, where he had been for less than six months. Baker had had a few skirmishes in Detroit as a teenager and then again just before he went off to college. Other than those few infractions, his record was clean."

"I don't see him as a very good candidate for espionage," John said to Klahan. "I had one of the security services check his banking records, and there is no indication that he is taking payoffs or anything else. Only the steady deposit of his monthly government checks was any indication of funds being put into his bank since he joined the Army."

"Well, he surely isn't saving for the future, according to the mama-sans at the Top of the Moon Massage Parlor in Cholon," Klahan said. "They say he comes into the parlor about twice a week for the complete treatment, if you know what I mean. I can tell you from experience that it is possible to spend several hundred dollars a visit to one of the more high-end parlors."

Baker was single, and he appeared to spend a lot of his income on entertainment, especially since he arrived in Saigon. There was no crime in that. However, if he were receiving funds illegally and running them through his checking account, that might indicate that he could be affiliated with those stealing and leaking the classified information and dealing in unsanctioned weapons trading.

"It's just simply not the case," John told Klahan as he pointed out Baker's financial statement for the last couple of years.

As John was looking over Beckers' classified file, however, something caught his eye. His background investigation came back fine, but his financials were somewhat disturbing. It appeared to John that large sums of money were being deposited into Beckers' account one day and then withdrawn the next day. John pulled out his calculator and added up the amount of funds in question. There was $120,000 deposited over the past six months and $120,000 withdrawn over that same period of time. There could be a simple explanation, but it might not be so simple. It could be a trust fund payment, although no indication in the major's file suggested that he was to receive from his family those amounts of funds. This was certainly a question that would need to be asked of the major when he was interrogated, and he would be interrogated. The money could be due to his cooperation with those who stole the classified information and somehow used the money to purchase illegal weapons and ship them back to the US. Everything considered, and as unlikely as it seemed impossible, MAJ Beckers had become the number one suspect.

Chapter 21

A Captain and a Major

"So, Mama-san," Klahan began. "Do you remember this G.I. coming to your parlor for the niceties of the house?" Klahan showed her a picture of CPT Baker and was looking for any signs that she knew of him. Many of the mama-sans that ran these flop houses were very discrete about their clientele because they wanted them to come back, and exposing them as regular customers was not considered a good business practice.

"Oh, yes, we know of this captain. He spends a lot of money, which is good, but he has beat up some of my girls, which is bad. We don't want him coming back into our parlor," she said with determination.

"Did any of your girls hear him bragging about his job or anything special that he does every day at the base?" Klahan asked.

"Oh, no," the mama-san said. "The only thing he bragged about was the size of his noodle!" And she laughed a good, hearty laugh at her response. "He's just a bully, and he knows we can't take any complaint of his treatment of the girls to the government since we are doing things for him that are not officially allowed. That's OK," she said with a slight grin. "We always win in the end, just like the sun and the moon. Some things never change in Saigon." With this parting comment, she bowed slightly to Klahan and closed the door.

Klahan reported back to John, and this information further clarified that the leak had to be coming from Beckers. "How do you propose to get MAJ Beckers to admit that he is the leak and share who else is involved? I would think that he would be afraid that whoever is doing all of this would try to harm him or his family if the ties go back to the US."

"Out of the mouth of babes." John slapped Klahan on the back. "You may have just helped clear up the 'why' of all of this."

Klahan stood looking at John as if he had two heads. "What in the hell are you talking about? If I'm so smart, please tell me why and how?"

"Well, Klahan," John said with a sly smile, "we are looking for a motive, a reason for MAJ Beckers to go off the reservation to make trouble for us, right?" he asked again to no one in particular. "Let's get our MAJ Beckers into the office and make him squirm a little to see if there is anything there to pursue as to his involvement in this blatant action against the US and ARVN forces. I will have the colonel summon him to his office for some other reason, and once we get him in the room, we will interrogate him."

"I like it," Klahan said. "Do you want to be the good cop or the bad cop?"

John looked at Klahan and just laughed out loud. "You've been watching too many late night movies, my friend. What we need to do is act like we know more than we do...let's let him prove he's innocent, rather than us proving he's guilty. If we were in a court of law, we couldn't do that, but when you are in the Army or other US Military organization, you really have no rights!"

"How soon do you think we can get the colonel to get that done?" Klahan asked John.

"How about right now?" John said and dialed the colonel's office.

"This is Colonel Forsett's office," a man's voice said. "How can I help you?"

"I need to speak to the colonel—it a matter of extreme urgency."

"May I tell him whose calling and what it concerns?"

"You can tell him that Bill Hicks is calling, and that it is important that I speak to him soon. I think you will find that he will want to speak to me immediately."

Moments later, the voice said, "Please hold for the colonel, Mr. Hicks."

"Is that you, Bill?" the colonel spoke into the telephone. "Do we need to meet?"

"Immediately, J.P. I don't want to discuss it over the phone. Should I come to your office, or should we meet somewhere else?"

"Let's meet at the Officer's Club. I will leave word at the door for you to be allowed into the hall. Say, twenty minutes?"

"Sure," he replied. "Please add Klahan's name to your visitor's list."

"Will do."

*　　*　　*　　*　　*

Twenty minutes later John and Klahan were entering the Officer's Club looking for the colonel. Once they gave their names to the guard at the door, they were immediately ushered into a small, private room, where they found the colonel seated in a comfortable chair and sipping bourbon on the rocks. He offered them a drink.

"Just a beer for me," Klahan said.

"Johnnie Walker Black for me," John replied.

Once they were seated in front of the colonel, they told him about the information that they had learned from the files of the four men they were following up on in regards to the information leak.

"So, what do you need from me, John?" the colonel asked.

"We need to get MAJ Beckers summoned to your office immediately under the guise of something other than this investigation. Any thoughts on how we can get that done?"

The colonel laughed a bit and said, "Well, the last time I checked, I was the commanding officer of this outfit. I don't need a reason to summon anyone to my office. How soon do you want him here?"

"Now, if possible," John answered. "We would like to interrogate him in your office, unless you can think of a better place to do something like that."

"My office is fine. I will have him there within the hour. You get there in the next forty-five minutes, and I will have the duty sergeant get you set up in a room that is suitable for that purpose."

"Sounds good, sir," John said.

Chapter 22

Major Beckers

Major Beckers was a little surprised to be called into the Old Man's office. He had been in the Vietnam theatre for over a year, and he had never been told to report to the C.O.'s office.

As Beckers came into the office of Colonel Forsett, he sized up the situation pretty quickly. This guy from the GAO office in Washington was there, along with some other people that he didn't know. Beckers asked Colonel Forsett, "Sir, is there something I can do for you?" assuming the colonel would be vague and weigh the situation before he answered the question.

"Well, Major," the colonel said with a bit of an edge to his voice. "There actually is something that you can do for me, and also for yourself. You can come clean about the $120,000 in cash that has been transferred into your checking account and then transferred out the very next day. This doesn't look good for you, MAJ Beckers, not good at all."

Major Beckers stood in front of the colonel's desk and simply mumbled a reply to the colonel's question. He didn't have a logical, legal explanation that he could use with the colonel, so he simply said nothing. Sometimes nothing was the best answer, because sharing too much information in the wrong hands could land you in Ft. Leavenworth or even worse, it could get you killed.

"Major," the colonel said impatiently, "I'm listening. What do you have to say for yourself? Right now, this looks really bad for you. You are implicated in multiple acts of espionage, each of which is punishable with sentences from ten to fifteen years in prison to the ultimate punishment of death by firing squad. If you have some light that you want to throw on the situation, now would be an excellent time to make that information available to Bill Hicks and his team. They are zeroing in on the details of the classified information being leaked and who is most likely involved in the cover-up. You are our number one suspect." Then the colonel said nothing to let the seriousness of the situation sink into the major's mind.

"It's not what you think, sir." Beckers started the conversation with a plea for understanding and a wish to explain his situation. "If I tell you what I know, my family will be hunted down and executed in the United States. If I don't tell you what I know, then I will be prosecuted for espionage and incarcerated for years to come, if not executed outright. I don't have much of a choice, and if I have to choose my family, then that's what I will do."

"Major, what makes you think your family will be safe if you don't come clean about the theft of these classified documents? What you don't understand is that you are a loose end and that whoever you are working with on the outside will eventually decide the risk is too great to let you live, no matter what you do to appease them. You need to get ahead of this thing."

John had been listening to this dialogue between the colonel and MAJ Beckers, and he saw a potential opening where he imagined the major would listen to some reason, even if he didn't see any way out of his troubles right now.

"Major," John began, trying carefully not to drive this officer whose career just took a definite turn for the worst over the edge of no return. "Let's look at this in a rational and non-emotional way. If you will help us stop this information leak that is compromising the entire US mainland, we will try to work out a way to get you into the witness protection program, along with your family."

Suddenly, the major broke down crying and tried to explain some of the reasons that he had shared the intelligence with the enemy. Before he started his story, John had told himself that there simply was not a good enough reason for anyone to commit an act of treason in a time of war.

Beckers said, "My wife and I have three children—one boy of eleven, and two girls, seven and five years old. My seven-year-old little girl," and with the mere reference to her, Beckers almost totally broke down and collapsed in his chair, "has been taken as a hostage to ensure that I continue to do whatever they need for me to do, or they have threatened to murder her." He was unable to continue.

"Get him a drink of whiskey," the colonel said to Klahan, who was standing nearby, transfixed by this horrible story of betrayal and kidnapping by a fellow American citizen. Klahan poured Beckers a shot of whiskey, and he gulped it down, hoping that it would calm his nerves. "Now, let's take a little break," the colonel said to John and Klahan and told the major to relax until the three of them talked about his predicament in private.

The colonel, John and Klahan stepped out of the interview room and into the colonel's office to confer about this new discovery.

"This is not good," John said to the colonel after they were sequestered back in the colonel's office. "Is there any way we can actually help him in his present situation? Espionage is punishable by death, right?"

"Surely, there is something that we can do to help this man and his family get out of this mess that they didn't create, isn't there colonel?" Klahan asked. "Isn't there some way to protect them from the bad people back in the States and still pursue the perpetrators here? There has to be a way around charging this man for treason—I wouldn't have done anything different had it happened to my family," Klahan said, almost angrily.

"It's not a matter of right and wrong, Klahan," the colonel began, "it is an oath soldiers, sailors, and airmen take to protect their country at all costs. It is a sacred oath, and it has been the benchmark of the staying power of our military people for centuries. If the Army made an exception for the major, then every time some unfortunate soldier gets in a bind, he would expect the same type of consideration, and that would weaken us in the field and overall morale could tumble. I think the only person who can grant such forgiveness is the President of the

United States, and this is such a hot potato that I don't think he would even want to come close to this situation," the colonel concluded.

"There is one way to make it happen, however, depending on how valuable his information is that he shares with us. Beckers can just disappear and be reunited with his family somewhere in America. I'm sure the CIA and FBI will be willing to help in any way they can if it means preventing large cashes of illegal weapons coming into the US and stemming the tide of information that is being siphoned off by the Viet Cong and NVA forces. Let me talk to the S-2 department in Washington and see if S-2 thinks that the CIA and the FBI will play along."

The colonel picked up his telephone and called the MPs, military police, to come and pick up the major and to hold him in a secluded place until Colonel Forsett heard back from Washington.

Chapter 23

Tu Thi Da'o

John knew that it would be at least tomorrow before the colonel would hear back from Washington about his proposal to let the major just disappear from Saigon and reappear somewhere else in the US, along with his family. He could see how the colonel would do whatever he had to do to save the major's young daughter, but the brass in Washington might not see things as clearly since they saw things some 9,000 miles away in a different world altogether. He would just have to wait until the colonel contacted him to move forward with his investigation. He thought it would be a good time to get some rest, have his special girl at the Steam and Cream Massage Parlor give him a massage and whatever they were willing to do to make him feel less stressed. He decided to head that way immediately. John said goodbye to Klahan at the office and made his way through the streets of Saigon to the parlor. He just kept telling himself that he needed to unwind.

Since John and Klahan were staying in the same building at night, they were able to talk over some strategy at the end of most days. This gave them both a feeling of comradery and sense that they were working even when they were off the clock, so to speak. He trusted Klahan about as much as anyone over here in 'Nam, and having a person to have your back in this kind of a place was absolutely necessary if you wanted to return home in one piece. Beyond the trust and the talent that he felt that Klahan brought to the table in these investigations, he actually began to think of him as a good friend.

Weeks earlier, John had become increasingly involved sexually and emotionally with a beautiful Vietnamese girl named To Thi

Da'o, who also worked and lived at the Steam and Cream Massage Parlor.

Da'o had grown up in Cholon and had attended a local Catholic school, where she had excelled in her studies of home economics. They had taught her to cook, manage a household, and she became an excellent seamstress. Prior to the Tet Offensive of 1968, Da'o had worked in a manufacturing plant in Saigon that created and made draperies for many of the elite residents of Saigon.

She had been working in the factory the day that the Viet Cong had overrun some of the city of Saigon and had just managed to escape from the plant before they burned it to the ground.

"I need to work for you," Da'o had told Tuyen a few months after she had lost her job at the plant. She had met Tuyen at the open air market in Saigon and had struck up a friendship with her just weeks before the fire. "I know that it involves having sex with American soldiers, but I don't know what else I can do to survive in the city."

Da'o came to work for her at the Magic Fingers Steam and Cream Massage Parlor and met Bill Hicks, the new GAO employee that had recently moved to Saigon from Washington, D.C.

"You treat me very nice," Da'o spoke to John in a soft, melodious voice. "I would like to be just your girl and not be with anyone else."

"I'm sure we can make that happen. I will make the arrangements with Tuyen so you can be my house-maid. You will have to take very special care of me. Can you do that?" he said with a wink.

"Oh, yes!" she said happily. "I will make sure you are a very happy man every day when you come home from work!" she said and lowered her eyes with an almost embarrassed grin.

When he would come home from work in the evening, she would undress him, bathe him in a huge tub in his room, and pleasure him in many ways commonly used by Asian women to please their men. He thought to himself that he could probably

79

just stay in this country after the war and enjoy the pleasures of Saigon's night life forever.

John had gone home to spend his evening with Da'o to relieve the unusual stress that he had been feeling since this manhunt had begun. When he arrived at the parlor, Tuyen was crying and jabbering in the Vietnamese dialect without appearing to take a breath. He finally got her to calm down enough and got her aside and asked her what had upset her so much.

"It's Da'o," she said, trying to hold back a flood of tears. "She has been murdered in your bedroom," she continued with a sad and mournful wail. "The Saigon city policemen were here and tried to say that you must have killed her, but I told them that you were not here all day. I think they finally believed me before they left. They said that they still wanted to speak to you about Da'o."

"How did this happen, Tuyen? Was anyone seen going in or coming out of our room today?" he asked rather helplessly. "I can't believe she has been taken from me." He began to howl with anger and sadness.

"There is something else," Tuyen told John in a whisper. "Before the local police came to investigate and carry her body away, I found a note written in English that said, 'Keep up this investigation, and everyone around you that you care about will die.' But the note was not signed," she whimpered through her tears. "I think the note was meant as a sign of warning for you. Da'o was such a beautiful and sweet girl," Tuyen said to John. "I can't believe that she is gone."

John knew that he would find the sons-of-bitches that did this to Da'o, and he would kill them with his bare hands, and he would do it very painfully and very slowly.

"Who would have a motive to kill a sweet girl like Da'o, and why did they want to get my attention?" John thought to himself. Obviously, he was getting too close for comfort for someone, and that someone had tried to dissuade John from continuing by murdering Da'o as an example of their power over him and his situation in Saigon. It would have just the opposite effect on

John, and it might give him more of a reason to take risks that he would never had guessed he was capable of when he was sitting nice and comfy in the air-conditioned apartment in Subic Bay.

This country was changing John, and although he knew it, he couldn't prevent the transformation from happening. Hurting from the hateful attack on Da'o, John focused now on his goal of making the Viet Cong or NVA pay for the life of Da'o. He would remember every aspect of that dreadful act so that he would never forget Da'o.

Chapter 24

Making the Best of a Bad Situation

The colonel's office contacted John and told him that he needed to see him right away. He was to report to Colonel Forsett within the hour and to bring Klahan with him.

John and Klahan walked into Forsett's office, and to their amazement, Major Beckers was sitting in one of the chairs across from the colonel, carrying on a civil conversation with him as if nothing had ever happened.

"Sir," John began, "can I assume that since the major is not in handcuffs or confined to his quarters that he has not been charged with a crime and is free to move about as if nothing has happened?"

"John," the colonel replied in a firm, but civil tone, "we have a situation that gives us the opportunity to make the best out of a really bad situation. No one, including the major, thinks that what he did is acceptable behavior, even if his family was being harassed and threatened to get him to cooperate with an organization that was operating counter to the wishes of this command and the directives of the Secretary of Defense in Washington. That being said, we have given the major an opportunity to help put things right." He looked directly at the major to ensure that Beckers understood that he had one opportunity to save his reputation and the lives of his family, as well as himself. The major nodded noticeably to all in the room, acknowledging the tough spot that he was in with all of these potential charges of espionage against him.

"So, Major Beckers," John calmly looked into his eyes as he questioned him, "how do you propose to convince us that you are on our side now, and not just saying things to save your own ass?"

"I assured Colonel Forsett that if the FBI can find my daughter and put my entire family in the Witness Protection Program, I will not only tell what I know about my part in this security leak, I will also help them and the CIA connect what is happening here with what is happening in the US and the AK-47 rifle influx into the country."

Colonel Forsett then added, "John, we have information that the FBI has located the major's daughter, and she will be in their custody, along with the rest of his family, in the next few days. We are expecting to see some indicators that some of the principal offenders, both here and in the US, will try to go underground to avoid detection and capture. We are willing to make the major disappear, as if he were lost in a skirmish or something of that nature, and he can then reappear in the US with his family in the Witness Protection Program and start his life over. The only condition for the CIA and FBI cooperation is that the major give us enough information to make it worth their efforts to make this happen for him. As soon as the FBI has secured the major's family, he will begin working with us to help us root out the real leak in our command," the colonel finished his thought and rose to get a glass of water from the sideboard in the office.

"Here's something you need to consider, Colonel," John said in a measured tone. "I have just come from my lodgings at the Steam and Cream Massage Parlor, and my girlfriend was murdered earlier today in our apartment. No one saw anyone come in or go out of the apartment, so the Saigon police want to talk to me about it. Tuyen told them that I was not home all day, and that seemed to have satisfied them for the moment, but they told her that they still wanted to talk to me. There was a note that was left in the room that she secured before the Saigon police arrived that threatened me and my friends if I didn't lay off this investigation. Now, to me, that doesn't seem like a Vietnamese tactic, but rather more of a mafia type threat with the evidence that they mean business by killing Da'o, my girlfriend, as an example to me that they can get to me or my friends at any time of the day or night. We have to assume that there are more people involved in this conspiracy than just Major Beckers."

"Oh, I can assure you that there are more people involved," the major chimed into the conversation. "I will gladly tell you all I know as soon as the FBI and CIA guarantee my safety and my family's safety," he repeated as if we had not heard him just a few minutes ago.

"Major," the colonel said with a very serious look on his face, "you are going to have to take it on good faith that we will do what we said we would do for you, but time is of the essence in this investigation. If we wait two or three more days until everything is in place to protect your family, and more people are murdered, or more weapons are discovered in the US, your deal will most likely disappear. Do you understand what I am trying to tell you?"

The major nodded his head and seemed resolved that he would have to trust the men in this room to do the right thing once he had shared all that he knew about the weapons for information scam.

Chapter 25

The Traitor is Exposed

Major Beckers began with the facts of the espionage that most affected him and his family. He had been in country for about three months when a high ranking person in the MACV office had approached him and asked if he would like to make a little extra money. He asked what the favor entailed and was told that all he needed to do as the communications officer was to give out some erroneous latitude and longitude information a couple of times and that it would be worth one thousand dollars for him. When he inquired why that kind of information would be worth so much money, he was told that answers to such questions were not important. All they wanted him to do is broadcast the new coordinates.

"I refused their offer," Beckers said, "but I should have reported the information to S-2 immediately. Instead I did nothing, thinking that since I did not play ball with them that everything would go away. As you know by now, it didn't go away. They began to threaten me personally, and I still would not help them. Finally, about four months ago I got a letter from my wife back home, and she told me that a couple of men came to the house and told her that she should tell me to cooperate with the people in Saigon, or some accident might happen to them at home. The next time I was approached, I played along thinking that I could find out what they were up to. To be honest with you, I had no idea that what I was doing was causing casualties or that it was linked to some weapons for guns deal. Of course, I suspected that it had to have something to do with smuggling or drugs or some other contraband, but I never found out what they were doing with the information. They deposited large sums of money in my bank account back home, and they moved it the next day somewhere else. I am as baffled about the money situation as you are, but I simply didn't know where to turn. I tried to quit helping them, and they took my youngest daughter and threatened to hurt her if I didn't continue to help them. I knew it was wrong at the time, but I feared for my daughter's life." The major picked up his glass of water and took a long pull of water before continuing. "They had a very influential NCO in the MAVC compound keeping tabs on me, so I couldn't alert the authorities."

"Do you know who that NCO is, Major?" the colonel demanded.

"Well, yes, sir. It's SGT Major Briggs, the 1st Sergeant of the battalion."

No one in the room was ready for that answer, especially Klahan. Klahan had confided everything to Briggs as if he were his father. The colonel had known Briggs for two years here in Saigon, but Briggs had a spotless military record with no blemishes, and he had the full cooperation and confidence of Colonel Forsett. Hell, he had the full cooperation and confidence of every officer and NCO in the whole city. How could this happen?

While the shock wave was still affecting those in the room, the major asked the colonel a simple question. "You know, sir, I was a little surprised that the SGT Major had immediately left for R&R yesterday. I just knew that he would be in your office as well. explaining his part in this whole thing."

"He did what?" the colonel roared.

"He left for Thailand for R&R yesterday, according to the duty officer. I thought you knew," the major continued. "The only reason that I know this for a fact is that I had planned to go to his office and tell him that I was going to confess to my part in this mess, but he was nowhere to be found. I later found out that he left yesterday morning for Bangkok."

The colonel picked up the phone and called for his office clerk to come into his office. "Who signed the R&R orders for SGT Major Briggs?" he blustered.

The clerk, a Specialist 4th Class, said with some confusion, "Well, you did, sir. I checked the signature before I printed off his pass to board the MAC flight to Bangkok yesterday. If you didn't sign it, sir, it must have been forged by SGT Major Briggs."

The colonel told the SP4 clerk to have all military police officers and intelligence officers in Saigon and Bangkok search for the SGT Major. He instructed him to have him arrested on suspicion of espionage if and when they encountered him. He also told them to consider him armed and dangerous and a suspect in a serious crime. With that, he put down his telephone and turned to John and Klahan.

"I suspect that Briggs may have been the catalyst of the murder of your girlfriend and co-worker. Now the pieces of the puzzle are falling into place. He would be able to find out who would be most vulnerable and dearest to you, John. He expected you to react as MAJ Beckers did and buckle under to his blackmail and threats. Once he received news that we were questioning everyone who had an opportunity to steal or mishandle the secret information in the secure office, he figured that the finger would eventually be pointed back at him. He fled to a US-friendly country to try to escape. We must move quickly, or he will slip through our security net and we might never find him again."

"Sir," John spoke to the colonel with a thoughtful gaze, "Klahan and I know the SGT Major on sight, but the other people looking for him don't really have a clue as to his appearance. He could alter his appearance just a little, and the MPs and others in pursuit of him might never spot him in disguise. Why don't you permit Klahan and me to go to Bangkok and see if we can help locate and apprehend him before he finds a way to leave the area and slip back into the US?"

"Excellent idea, John." However, you have a big grudge to settle with Briggs after he caused the death of your girlfriend, and

I don't want any vigilante justice with Briggs. Can you promise me that you will resist taking matters into your own hands if I let you go after him?"

John looked the colonel in the eyes, and with a serious look on his face he said, "Yes, Colonel, I can let the government punish him. However, if he doesn't get the proper discipline by the Justice Department, I will personally become his judge, jury and executioner!" With that statement, John simply saluted the colonel and left his office without speaking another word to anyone.

PART II: A MAN ON THE RUN

Chapter 26

All Good Things Must End

Daniel Briggs was on the run. He knew that his gravy train at MACV would eventually come to a screeching halt, and he had made contingency plans to move his operation away from Saigon once it became no longer feasible to operate in the open in Saigon. He had been working with mercenaries for a couple of years in Vietnam, but that new lieutenant from Subic Bay fouled everything up when he landed in country. Of course, Briggs knew that all Bremen was doing was following Colonel Forsett's orders, but it still pissed him off that he would have to work around this new wrinkle in his plan to ship weapons for information back to the US. He had a good thing going with Beckers because Beckers was weak and could be manipulated; not so with Lieutenant John Bremen. He had thought that he could influence Bremen effectively by hiring Klahan.

Without knowing that he was aiding and abetting Briggs, Klahan had effectively been Brigg's eyes and ears on what John was doing and how far along the investigation into the weapons for information had progressed. So, when Klahan had said recently that they were getting ready to investigate those four on the security leak issue, Briggs knew it was time for him to get ready to make his move.

Briggs tried to slow down the investigation by killing that little geisha girl that John Bremen was shacking up with in the massage parlor. However, it looked like it had the opposite effect. Once they arrested that wimp Beckers, Briggs would only have a short period of time before they put it all together and came after him. That fucking Bremen was a Boy Scout—that's for sure. He needed to serve in Vietnam for a year or two, and he would begin to see that there was no black-and-white—no right and wrong. There were only shades of grey.

"That's okay," Briggs thought to himself. "By the time they figure out where I have gone, they will have a hard time tracking me down." He chuckled to himself and opened another beer. The flight to Bangkok would be landing in an hour, and he was ready to put phase two of his plan into action.

Briggs had been stealing information and trading it for AK-47 Chinese Communist rifles for more than two years, and he had done it right under Colonel Forsett's nose. That self-righteous son-of-a-bitch had been preaching about loyalty, God and country, the American way, and other bullshit for so long that Briggs had come to know the speeches by heart.

However, Forsett was not opposed to turning a blind eye to things that he benefited from as a commander. Forsett also managed to get several contraband items shipped back to the US, and he never felt guilty about it because who was going to question his actions? No one had the balls to question Forsett on anything. To Briggs, stealing was stealing. And his philosophy was that if he was going to steal anything, he would make it worth his while. Briggs had not planned for this weapons for information gig to happen. It was so coincidental that he ever got hooked up with his dealer back in the US that he still marveled at the fact that they had made the connection at all.

Briggs had been on his annual leave back in Dallas, Texas, when he ran into a distant cousin of his from high school. Jimmy Garrison was Briggs' second cousin on his father's side. After a few minutes of catching up on old times, his cousin Jimmy asked him, "Hey, Danny, tell me what you actually do over there in rice patty land?"

"Well, basically, I supervise all of the operations of a large military base in the Saigon area. It's really not much different than managing some commercial business here in Texas."

"Boy, I'd sure like to get my hands on one of those bad-ass AK-47 rifles that I have heard so much about. Do you think you could somehow get me one and get it shipped here without either of us getting into trouble over it?"

Brigg's first and automatic response to such a question was always a resounding "no." However, he gave this a little thought. "What do you think someone would be willing to pay for something like that if I could get some of those shipped over here?"

"I don't know, but I'll bet you could almost name your price," Jimmy answered.

"Well, Jimmy, it depends on what you have to trade for one in Vietnam. Sometimes they will trade you an AK-47 for a bowl or rice or a good, dry place to sleep at night," Briggs said. "Why would you want a weapon like that anyway? They are made for war."

Without hesitation, Jimmy said, "That's what we have here in the 'hood and between the crime syndicate families...war. I could make a killing on some of those rifles. Can you get lots of ammunition to go with them?"

"If we can find a source for the rifles, we can find a supply of rounds of ammo," Briggs replied. "How many do you think you could sell if I could somehow get them to you?"

"Fifty thousand to start," Jimmy said without blinking an eye. "We could sell another 5,000 to 10,000 a month after that."

"And who do you plan to sell them to once you have them here in the US?" "You see, it's like this," Jimmy continued, "we would sell the first batch to the crime bosses and gangs who are currently using Thompson machine guns. The Thompson has good stopping power, but you have to get up close to use it effectively. But I have heard that the range on the AK-47 is up to 800 meters. That's damn near half a mile. So, you can hold off your enemy for a long time while you're getting your business done or just trying to get away," he said with an excited tone in his voice. "Is that true about their range?" he asked to confirm what he had heard on the street.

"That's probably a good estimate of the maximum range of the rifle," Briggs continued, "but it is only probably really effective up to 250 meters."

"Even at that distance, you're looking at a couple of city blocks. That's a hell of a lot of firepower in a city setting, Danny," Jimmy went on. "Give me a price on what you think you would have to charge to get them here, ready to go with the ammunition."

"Around $200 per rifle, that's assuming that I can find that many available and can figure out a way to smuggle them into the country without getting caught. You would have to wire money to an offshore account to make it work. Could you arrange that if I can get the weapons?"

"Hell, yeah," he said. "How soon do you think you can get the first shipment to us?" Jimmy was almost bubbling over with excitement.

"I'll have to get back to Saigon and figure out the logistics of how to find them, how to get them from the Viet Cong or NVA troops, and then how to get them to you. It would be considered a traitorous act if anyone can trace the weapons cache back to me or my people. I will have to send you the information back from Saigon once I figure everything out. Give me your address and telephone number. Almost all of the telephone calls and all of the mail that comes in and out of Saigon are screened by an intelligence group to make sure that no one is compromising classified information from the command. We will need to have a code that I can give you over the telephone. We can communicate by way of the US Postal Service as well."

"We will use this type of code. If it's a 'go' or 'yes,' we could send a message like, 'It's raining like a cow pissing on a flat rock.' If it's a 'no-go' or not going to happen, it could be something like 'send the candy you promised me in your last letter,' or something to that effect. If we use the same phrases that the guys use on a daily basis to communicate with each other there, then there is no way anyone will catch on to our code."

"That's fucking genius," Jimmy said as he slapped Briggs on the shoulder. "Figure out a set of code sentences and make sure I have a copy before you leave to go back to Saigon, and we can do our business right under the government's nose, and no one will be the wiser. I'll start putting out my feelers to see how many rifles I can move when they get here. Just check back with me before you return to Saigon."

As they headed off in separate directions, Briggs did a little quick math in his head and was pleased that he had finally found a way to get the US Government to pay him back for all of the years he had served his country without the benefit of real financial security. "Fifty thousand rifles x $200 = $1,000,000 on the first order alone," he thought greedily. "Even with the cost of bartering something with the Vietnamese for the rifles, I can put at least $500,000 in an offshore account as a nest egg that I will need once I leave the service." He would figure all of that out when he got back in country, but for now he needed to create the password phrases for Jimmy before he lost his courage to take on the US Government. This Vietnamese War was becoming a favorite pastime for Briggs.

*   *   *   *   *

Once Briggs got back to Saigon, he was able to find a mercenary soldier who hooked him up with a supplier of AK-47 rifles. He had to agree to trade classified information to the guy for the weapons, but he figured that it wouldn't hurt if it was something as simple as coordinates on a map. Obviously, he had figured incorrectly, and as time went by he had to plan an exit strategy from Saigon and the US Army.

Chapter 27

Planning for the Big Exit

About a year ago, Briggs had taken an R&R to Singapore and opened an account at the OCBC, the Overseas-Chinese Bank Corporation. He transferred all the money he had been accumulating into that numbered account. He had accumulated well over one million US dollars, and he had several more payments that he expected to come into the account in the next few weeks. This money would be his safety blanket once his actions were discovered. He was a realist. He knew it wasn't whether or not his treachery would be discovered, but rather when it would happen. Now, he was ready for phase two of his plan.

When Briggs took the MAC flight from Tan Son Nhut, he didn't do anything to hide his identity. He actually wanted the agents and military police to see him boarding an airplane bound for Bangkok. Over ten million people lived in the greater Bangkok metropolitan area, and he knew he could hide there long enough to move on to his real hideaway in Japan. However, he would stay in the city of Bangkok long enough to be seen by enough people in the US Government agencies to convince them that Bangkok was his final destination. They would continue looking for him for an indefinite period of time, which should give him ample time to get hunkered down in his new identity and his new hiding place in Kumamoto, Japan.

Kumamoto was large enough to get lost among the people on the street, but it was small enough to be able to operate freely without the Japanese Government getting too nosy. He didn't want to arouse any suspicions for any reason. He was going to simply be an American expatriate who decided to settle down and retire in a nice, serene city in the Orient. He had secured identity papers as "Joseph Romano" six months ago—a local Japanese driver's license and a Japanese passport with his new identity. He had even purchased a bungalow in the outskirts of Kumamoto through a real estate agent three months earlier. He would simply "come home" from an overseas trip, and none would be the wiser. He had to hand it to himself—he was one smart cookie!

The only thing that Briggs had not pre-planned was how to get from Bangkok to Kumamoto. He didn't want the CIA to be able to trace his journey by subpoenaing records of all travel agencies to determine how he escaped Bangkok, so he simply decided to wait until he got to Thailand to negotiate his travel to Kumamoto. He had converted some US Dollars into Yen and Thai Bahts two months ago just after Colonel Forsett had begun the investigation into the security leak. He made sure he would have ample Yen until he reached Kumamoto, and he figured he would need enough Thai Bahts for several days of travel and lodging around the city of Bangkok. If the colonel had not included him in the plan to find the security leak, he could have been discovered and arrested before he could put his escape plan into action.

Now, he was simply looking for the best way, not necessarily the fastest or cheapest way, to travel to Kumamoto without being discovered. He had been in the Army for many years, and he knew that the best way to find out things that were operated outside of the military's sanctioned control was to visit a local bar and keep his ears open and his mouth shut. That's exactly what he intended to do. Fortunately, for Briggs, he had checked out several sea-going vessels in advance of his trip to Bangkok, and he figured someone at the docks would be able to speak enough English to help him determine which ship to take to Japan and whom to trust getting that task completed. He picked out several bars near the dock area and began his chore of choosing the right vessels.

Briggs walked into a rather seedy looking bar named the Pig 'N Whistle near the docks and looked around to size up the clientele.

Just as he had figured, it was a typical dive where drunks and smugglers would tend to hang out between more productive times. He thought he might have just found a way to connect with discrete transportation out of Bangkok, and he knew the way to test his theory. Waving the cocktail waitress over and giving her a US ten dollar bill, Briggs asked, "Do you speak any English?"

She responded, "Yes, some. What can I get you to drink?"

"Bourbon and water on the rocks," he said. "By the way, I am looking for a boat to take me to Japan. Do you know who I can speak to about something like that?"

She nodded and went away to get his drink. A few minutes later, a somewhat burly Thai sailor came and sat down at his table.

"Buy me a drink?" the sailor inquired of Briggs without really looking him straight in the eye.

"Sure," Briggs replied and waved the cocktail waitress back over to his table. "What would you like? This young lady will get your drink for you."

"I'll have a whiskey neat. So, I hear you want to go to Japan, Yes? Where in Japan do you want to go? There are many ports in Japan, my friend. What's your name?"

"Joseph Moreno," Briggs said and showed his driver's license and US passport to the sailor.

"And where would you like to go, Mr. Moreno?"

"Onomichi, Yawathahama, Iwakuni, or anywhere in the southern region of the Japanese Islands."

"Wouldn't it be easier and faster for you to fly there instead of taking a ship?" the sailor continued. "Why would you want to spend several days on a freighter when you could fly there in a matter of hours for less money?"

"I have my reasons," Briggs said. "So, can you make that happen, and if so, how much will it cost me?"

"Three hundred dollars, cash, and another three hundred once you reach the port. You can probably fly there for a couple of hundred dollars if the price is too steep for you," the sailor said with a twinkle in his eye. He didn't know what this American was running away from, and he really didn't care, but whether he was a deserter, a criminal or just someone who didn't like flying, he would make the most of the situation.

"Sounds fair," Briggs replied, "and when do we leave port?"

"We leave tomorrow morning at daylight. Be at dock 12A at 5:00 AM if you want to go with us. We have decent accommodations on board, but it's not a luxury ship."

"I will be there."

The sailor downed his drink and left without so much as looking back at Briggs as he left the bar.

*　　*　　*　　*　　*

The next morning, Briggs met the sailor at Dock 12A, boarded the vessel, and got settled into his quarters below. It was a three-day trip, and the accommodations were acceptable, but it was definitely not the *Queen Elizabeth*. He would arrive in Iwakuni in about three days, and he would have to reassess his weapons for intelligence scheme that would now have to be run out of Japan, assuming he didn't just decide to take what profits he had already made and count himself lucky. He had three days to decide what he was going to do, and the three bottles of bourbon that he had brought with him would help him make that crossing a little less painful.

Chapter 28

An Evasive SGT Major in Bangkok

"We have tracked Briggs to Bangkok," Officer of the Day Captain Ralph Harrelson reported to Colonel Forsett. "We know he landed yesterday on a MAC flight out of Tan Son Nhut sometime around 3:00 PM. Our local intelligence sources have spotted him in the market-place and visiting several stores and bars, including the Windsor Hotel. They lost sight of him sometime this morning after being spotted in downtown Bangkok catching a taxi ride to who knows where. What would you like us to do, sir? Do you want us to put out an all-points bulletin with the local police, or do you think that might cause more chaos than be helpful? I know we have to be diplomatic in our approach since Thailand is an ally and not directly under our military influence like Saigon."

The captain assumed the colonel would indeed put out an APB on this character, and he was surprised when the colonel said, "No, let's try to locate him first. We don't need an international incident on our hands. We need to clean this up nice and tidy without alerting the local media that we have a very high ranking NCO on the run who is possibly a traitor to boot!"

The colonel picked up his shot glass and knocked back a drink of liquor. "Just keep me in the loop, Captain," he said and left his office for the day.

*   *   *   *   *

John Bremen and Klahan arrived in Bangkok the morning after Briggs had arrived the previous afternoon. They checked in with the CIA operatives that they were connected with in Thailand and were brought up to date on everything that was known about

Briggs and his movements since he had touched down in Bangkok the day before. Having been there for a couple of weeks on R&R, John and Klahan were somewhat familiar with the city and the places where Briggs would hide until he made his move to go underground.

"It's like looking for a needle in a haystack," John said to Klahan. Klahan looked at John with enough perplexity that John finally figured out that Klahan had no idea what that homespun saying meant. So, he tried to explain it to him.

"See," he began with Klahan, "back in the States, someone might say, 'It's like finding a needle in a haystack,' which means it is damn near impossible to accomplish that particular task. Do you understand now?"

"Why would you want to put a needle in a haystack and then look for it, John? That seems like a waste of time to me. I imagine it would be almost impossible to find, yes?"

"OK, Klahan. Let's just forget that idiom for the time being," John said. "Look, with nearly ten million people in the Metropolitan Bangkok area, we will not find Briggs by just walking around the city like tourists. We need a lead. We need to ask ourselves, 'What would I do if I were trying to hide from the authorities in a city as large as Bangkok?' So, we start with the flop joints, sleazy bars and hotels and go from there. Does that make sense to you?"

"Sure. But do we go about narrowing down our search area, so we are not wasting time looking in places that Briggs probably would not go?" Klahan asked.

"Since Thailand is an ally, they will want to help us, to a degree, because they will not want the US Government putting Bangkok on a restricted area list, which would hurt the local economy a lot. We just need to ask them nicely to be helpful in our search. They can tell us in fifteen minutes what would take us two weeks to learn."

"That makes sense to me," Klahan said. "So I guess we go to the local police station and begin our search there?"

"Not just yet, Klahan. I think we start with the local CIA operatives here and move our investigation along as we get more feedback from the dives where we look for him and the messages that Colonel Forsett sends us. He can't just 'disappear' altogether. However, it is important that we work quickly because once his trail gets cold, we will probably never find or catch him."

John and Klahan checked into a local hotel in the sleazier part of Bangkok. They wanted to put the odds in their favor that Briggs might make a mistake that could blow his cover and make him an easier target for them to find. Tomorrow was another day, and John and Klahan both were asleep in less than five minutes after their heads hit their pillows.

Chapter 29

The Great Escape

Klahan and John decided that they would use a normal protocol to try and locate Briggs and determine whether he left the city or even left Thailand altogether. It would not be easy since there were numerous ways Briggs could have made himself disappear in a city the size of Bangkok. First and foremost, they would ask the local police to work with the CIA branch in Bangkok to survey all American or European born travelers as they attempted to cross the borders into Laos or Cambodia.   Next, they decided to determine how a person might try to disappear themselves from a city of ten million people. The logical thing was to visit the airlines and shipping docks to see if anyone fitting Brigg's description had sought out or found a way to leave Bangkok without being detected by the civil authorities.

Klahan took the airlines, and John took the docks where the ships were moored. They had agreed to meet at 2 PM at the Rajah Hotel to compare notes. After going over all of the data that they had gathered so far, they determined that Briggs must have planned this getaway for some time to not leave any traces of his disappearance in Bangkok. They had not given up hope finding Briggs, but it appeared to them that they might actually be trying to find out where he went rather than preventing him from escaping.   Either way, it was quite evident that Briggs was running, and that fact alone reinforced their earlier suspicion that he was in deep with the security problem back at MACV.

"So, John, what do you want to do now?" Klahan asked. "We have pretty much run out of leads. Even the scarce leads we had have proven totally useless. I guess we could backtrack over all that we have discovered to see if we missed something. Surely, this guy couldn't have just disappeared into thin air, could he?"

John was scratching his head and trying to think to himself what he could have missed in their pursuit of Briggs. "You know, I think the old SGT Major has been cooking this plan up for some time. Although we couldn't have known it at the time, he probably began activating his escape plans once he saw that we were zeroing in on Beckers. It only makes sense because this plan of his could not have been pulled off so smoothly if he had just decided to flee Saigon a day or two ago. It appears to me that a lot of planning has gone into whatever he has done to make himself undetectable."

"We are definitely missing something here," Klahan joined in on the synopsis of Briggs' escape plan. "Maybe we are going about this all wrong. Maybe he just came to Bangkok with money in his pocket and an ultimate destination in mind. If so, how do we go about getting into his head and finding out where that destination could be?"

"I think we need to go back to Saigon and talk this thing through with Colonel Forsett," John said. "There has to be something in his recent past that could be an indicator of where he is headed. We will alert the CIA desk in Saigon while we are heading back to base, so they can be working up a background on all of his communications, banking info, and other personal data that might be helpful in giving us some leads to pursue. Right now, I've got nothing but questions!"

Across town at the harbor where Briggs was waiting patiently for his ship to set sail for Japan, he was feeling pretty damn good about his ability to slip the CIA and Forsett's henchmen and be on his way to his secret hideout. What was worrying him was not the probability of getting caught right now, but rather how he was going to be able to conduct his illicit business some 2100 miles from Saigon and not have his partners lose confidence that he could still deliver the goods.

Chapter 30

Sergeant Almandinger

Tuyen was still waiting on Klahan and the colonel to help her find out who had destroyed her beloved Hue and killed her family. Although Klahan had helped John root out the leak that Beckers had been perpetrating in his position as communications officer, he had not made any real inroads on getting information for them concerning their families in Hue. She had been coaching her girls for some time to question every soldier who came into the parlor about whether or not they had been in or around the Hue area when the Tet Offensive was going on. So far, she had a few leads, but nothing substantial enough to lead them to who killed their families or why they were targeted by the Viet Cong.

They had a pretty good idea why, but if they were going to receive justice for their families, they needed more facts before they could move forward and try to find and destroy the murderers. Klahan had called Tuyen from Bangkok and told her that he would be home later that day, and she had decided that she would try to inspire him to resume their search in Hue. Although she had not had much success learning from the soldiers who had been in Hue, there was one sergeant who had been on the scene the day of the Battle of Hue, and he had some information that Klahan might be able to pursue with the Americans. She wrote down Terry Almandinger's contact information for Klahan, so she could give it to him when he arrived home from his trip to Bangkok.

When Klahan and John arrived back in Saigon, they stopped by Colonel Forsett's office just long enough for him to debrief them, and then they decided they would return home to the Magic Fingers Parlor. They were both very tired from their whirlwind trip to Bangkok, and all they really wanted to do was get some sleep and start all over in the morning. However, Tuyen had another idea and began to tell Klahan all about her visit with Almandinger and the information that he had shared with her on his last visit to the parlor.

"I don't know if it is enough information to get us started with the Americans, but it's worth a chance if you can get the colonel to help us. He owes you, Klahan, for all of the help you have given him helping him figure out who his bad guys were in the security leak situation," Tuyen said. "Will you please at least ask him if he will help us?"

"Yes," he said with sadness in his eyes for Tuyen's continuing sorrow as she thought about her family and how it all had changed her life. "I will speak to him tomorrow. John and I have to go back to the colonel's office and fill out some reports about our trip to Bangkok, so I will ask the colonel while I am with him how he might help us find out more about this SGT Almandinger's commanding officer during the raid, and if he can shed some light on the motive for killing our entire families."

Chapter 31

Cousin Jimmy the Hoodlum

Jimmy Garrison wasn't just any old cousin of Briggs. He was an up and coming soldier in the crime family located in the Dallas area. He had paid his dues just like every soldier before him; knocking off small-time jewelry stores, getting started in the collection portion of the business, and eventually becoming a captain in his Uncle Salvatore's organized crime army. Uncle Salvatore Antillo had been the Don in Houston until he was replaced by the family and run out of town. Uncle Salvatore settled in Dallas and became a very important member of the mob, with connections all over the Northeast and South. When the average person saw him on the street, he had no idea of the connections that Salvatore still had with the mob. He did a pretty good job keeping a low profile, and the word was out that he was a made man, and no one was going to touch Uncle Salvatore.

Jimmy Garrison was another thing altogether when it came to crime. He was an up and coming player who wanted to make his presence known all around and his potential to actually run a piece of the crime syndicate. He knew that three things mattered in the family—loyalty, perceived power, and finally, being feared by his competitors. Jimmy had worked for Uncle Salvatore long enough to know that you kept your button men and soldiers on a short leash. His job was to set the course for the family, and those who answered to him were expected to carry out the mission whether they thought it was a good idea or not. And what a break he had gotten a couple of years ago when Cousin Danny was visiting on leave from Vietnam!

Who would have thought that he would be in a position to make the kinds of powerful deals with the families in New York, Miami, and San Francisco that he was now doing now? This was really going to make him a made man in Dallas. Since Uncle Salvatore was a made man, he could recommend his nephew, and Jimmy had completed the most serious prequalification by killing a rival button man for another family in Jersey.

Everyone knew that Uncle Salvatore's family had deep Italian roots, and without that pedigree no one could become a made man in the Mafia. What Jimmy had to make absolutely certain was that the scheme that he and Cousin Danny had cooked up to get AK-47 rifles into the country and into his family's distribution system was going to be a steady supply source. Otherwise, his position of prestige and power would be only a temporary one. Now that Danny had been funneling weapons to Jimmy for the past year and a half, Jimmy's position was strong in the family business. It was about the time that his cousin would be contacting him about the next shipment, and it was a good thing since demand had doubled for the AK-47s in the last few months.

Chapter 32

Setting a Trap for Briggs

"Tuyen, I will ask the colonel this morning if he can put me in touch with the commanding officer of the unit where SGT Almandinger is assigned and see if we can find out more about the battle that took our families away from us. I spoke with John on the way back from Bangkok, and he is willing to help us since I helped him uncover his thief and traitor," Klahan said. "We will get right on it as soon as we are finished with the follow up with the colonel on this Briggs thing."

"Thank you, Klahan," she said. "I will feel so much better once we have figured out if there is anything we can do to honor the memory of our families." She was getting more excited as every small detail of what had happened in Hue began to build into a plausible and logical sequence of events. They might actually be able to find out enough details to go after whoever caused this misery for both of them.

*   *   *   *   *

John was at the office when Klahan arrived, and they both looked rested from a good meal, a hot bath, a good woman, and a good night's sleep. The colonel was less than happy that they had not been able to detect how and where Briggs had escaped from Bangkok.

"I'm not going to make any excuses, sir," John told the colonel, "but by the time we arrived, I suspect that Briggs had already left the immediate area of Bangkok, or possibly even Thailand. It appears from the way he was able to leave the area without leaving a trace that his escape plan of his was well-thought out and not something he put together at the last minute. Had any of us suspected him, he wouldn't have had the time to work out such a successful exit from the area."

"Well, John," said Forsett, "we would never have suspected a highly decorated and presumably loyal and honest NCO to turn traitor on us. It just never crossed my mind that something like that could happen. Wildest thing I've ever seen in my entire military career, and I've seen a lot of shit happen! What we really need to address is how much damage that son-of-a-bitch has done to this command and to our country back home. We may never know the full extent of that damage, but I think we need to try and track down as much information about things as we can and pass it along to the Pentagon."

"Let me make a suggestion, sir," Klahan broke into the conversation. "It may be a good thing to let Briggs and his conspirators think that they have gotten away with it and that we are not going to pursue them just long enough to get them to let their guard down, and then we might find the search for them easier. Briggs will have a hard time totally walking away from it all when there is still a lot of money to be made trading weapons for information and cash."

"So, Klahan, what do you have in mind?" asked the colonel.

"Tuyen and I have discovered a lead that puts a sergeant at the battle when Hue was destroyed and our families were murdered. John has volunteered to help me root out some of the potential information that may be available from that sergeant or from his commander. The sergeant's name is Terry Almandinger, and we need to find out who his commanding officer was when Hue was attacked. He may not can help us, but it's worth a try."

"And, if Briggs is as smart as I think he probably is, he may think that we are going about our search in a totally different direction from him. In the meantime, we can work with various offices of the CIA in countries surrounding Thailand to see if anyone has spotted him in transit. What do you think of the diversion, sir?"

109

Without answering Klahan, the colonel asked John directly. "So, what do you think of Klahan's plan? Do you think it will work to disguise what we are going to be doing to run down Briggs?"

John said thoughtfully, "You know, sir, it could just be the thing we can do to throw him off his guard while we are tracking him down for the kill. The CIA can track down every phone call and piece of mail Briggs has received for the last two years, if necessary, and we will definitely generate some leads that way. The way I see it, Colonel, we owe Klahan to help him and Tuyen try to find the cowards that killed their families. They have both worked with us to help us discover the MACV security leak, and they need our help to move forward looking into their own private nightmares."

"OK, then. It's settled. I will give you guys two weeks to work on the Hue affair, and then I will need you both back on this continuing problem we have with Briggs and his partners. Do you think you can get that done in two weeks?"

"We don't have much choice, do we, sir?" John answered the colonel.

Klahan add confidently, "We will get it done, sir."

"OK," the colonel said. "See you in two weeks, and good luck!"

Klahan was very excited about the unilateral support that the colonel had shown him in regards to his ongoing search for the culprits who caused all of the mayhem in Hue. He knew, beyond a doubt, that Tuyen would be thrilled beyond words to know that the American Government was not only going to allow them to search for the killers, but that they would also help them find and punish them. It was more than she had hoped for, and when Klahan told her the full story, she hung her head and wept silently.

Chapter 33

Getting Closure for Tuyen

John and Klahan contacted SGT Almandinger in Da Nang and spoke with him about the day his unit had fought in the Hue area. Almandinger said that it appeared to his unit commander that the Viet Cong was not just trying to harm the infrastructure of the city, but that they were going on a house-to-house search looking for specific individuals for punishment or elimination. They thought this was true because some of the people in high political and business positions were murdered, along with their entire families, while some were simply ignored and passed over.

According to SGT Almandinger, one of the officers in the Viet Cong Army was interrogated, and he told them that those people were being punished for crimes against the state and for commiserating with the American forces and the South Vietnamese Government. The Viet Cong officer said that his commanding officer had given them a list of people to target, but he could not remember who was on the list. It was a specific number of people and not just a random assignment to kill citizens when they invaded Hue.

Almandinger also told John and Klahan that the commander who gave those orders was killed in the battle, and the intelligence died with him. Even though Klahan knew that Tuyen would not be totally happy with this information, at least it would give her some closure on the situation so she could move on with her life as well. Klahan and John went back to Saigon and sat down with Tuyen to explain everything to her so she could come to the realization that they had discovered all of the facts that were available about why their families were killed during the battle at Hue. Klahan hoped the information would be enough to give her some closure because it had provided that for him.

Amazingly, when John and Klahan were in Da Nang seeking out SGT Almandinger, they heard rumors and stories of one of the NVA units running an undercover operation trading AK-47s for credible information on the movements of US and ARVN troops.

"Do you think this may have been one of the contacts that Briggs had used to secure the weapons that he smuggled out of this country to the USA?" Klahan asked John.

"It could well have been, Klahan. Let's do a little more digging into the good sergeant's past when we get back to MACV headquarters and see if we can make a connection of any kind linking Briggs to the AK-47 trading scheme that helped take down Hue."

This sounded like a good idea to both of them. Such information might even lead John to the murderer of his Da'o. John had vowed in his heart that if he discovered who had killed Da'o, he would kill that person himself. Plans for his own personal revenge on that person had not changed and would not change, assuming John got the chance.

Chapter 34

Briggs in Kumamoto

Briggs was finally settling into his new lifestyle in Kumamoto. It had taken a few days to slip into his new identity, but he thought it was working out pretty well for him now. It had been a couple of weeks since he had evaded the colonel's hit men, along with the CIA in Thailand, but in the long run he had won that battle, as he had expected to do from the beginning.

"Let's face it," Briggs thought to himself, "I'm much smarter than any of those CIA guys. They are not nearly as good as their reputation would make out that they are." He laughed to himself and decided that it was time for him to contact his cousin back in Texas to begin shipping AK-47s to them again. It was just too good of a thing for him to let it go simply because he had become incognito to stay out of the US Government's reach.

The system that Briggs had put into place in Saigon was now exposed, along with Beckers as well as the blackmail that was going on between the crime family and the abduction of Beckers' daughter. It would be a lot more difficult to make it worthwhile for the mercenaries to supply weapons to Briggs now that his communication's officer could not secretly inform them of when and where the American and ARVN patrols would be at any particular time. It wasn't an impossible feat, but it would be more difficult.

The first thing Briggs needed to do was to contact Jimmy Garrison and renegotiate the fee for the weapons. It would cost considerably more to find, consign, and ship the AK-47s since Briggs would no longer have the cover of the US Government to ship the weapons back to America without danger of the containers being inspected more closely. Also, the mercenaries would know that Briggs had lost his influence and power, and once they detected a weakness in his situation, they would leverage that situation against him. What Briggs needed to do first and foremost was to determine if all of the changes that he would have to make to keep shipping weapons to Jimmy in American were actually worth it to him.

"First things first," he thought to himself. He needed to get Jimmy on board with all of the necessary changes, or he would just drop off the face of the Earth with anyone who knew him before he was outed by the CIA in Saigon. It was not what he had planned for his final swan song with the US Army, but he guessed it would have to do. Jimmy was not aware that the situation in Saigon had changed and that the supply link for the weapons was going to have to change as well. He would have to think through the necessary changes in his smuggling infrastructure before he alerted his cousin on the changes.

Briggs was thinking back over some of the low-life NCOs in his command in Saigon to see if there was a way to get some help from the inside since both he and Beckers were no longer operating in the Vietnam theatre to be hands-on to make something of this magnitude work. It took a while for him to come up with a name because he had simply transferred anyone in the unit away if he was a threat to him achieving the highest scores on his regular Inspector General visits, which happened at least once a year. Now, he wished he had kept a list of those troublemakers. A troublemaker with a sense of greed is what he needed most right now.

What was that kid's name who had been in trouble in New York City who was given the choice of joining the service or going to prison for ten years? He thought long and hard and came up with the name Lewis Barett.

*   *   *   *   *

Lewis was definitely a fuck up. He had been caught on numerous occasions in petty larceny situations back in Chicago, and once he turned eighteen years old the punishment went from juvenile retention centers to spending the night in jail with the hardened criminals. He was definitely on a path that would lead him to forced incarceration at a major prison facility. The judge who oversaw most of his cases took pity on the kid and gave him the option of joining the Army or going away for five to ten years to serve hard time. Lewis might have been larcenous and a bit amoral, but he was not stupid. He was at the US Army recruitment center the next morning with his probation officer.

"Why, of course, we would love for Mr. Barett to be a part of the US Army!" the recruiter said as he slapped Lewis on the back and motioned for him to sit down and begin filling out the paperwork for the induction. This one was almost too easy for the recruiter. And, he thought to himself, "I'm getting paid to do this. Isn't America great?" He chuckled as he checked one more required recruit for that month off his status report.

Recruiters had to make their quota every month with fresh new recruits, or they could be reassigned to another tour of duty in Southeast Asia. This goofy kid was the answer to a prayer by the recruiter, and he got Lewis to sign the register for immediate induction into the US Army.

After his mandatory eight weeks of basic training at Ft. Jackson, S.C., Lewis was assigned to clerk typist school. This meant that most likely he would be assigned to a unit behind the lines so he could construct the morning report documents or the sick call lists. There was no question in anyone's mind where his first duty station would be once he finished all his basic schooling. He would be on his way to Vietnam within six months of joining the US Army. Actually, Lewis didn't mind thinking about Vietnam as a duty assignment. He had heard that his money would go a long way toward getting drunk and banging the local women. Not a bad assignment for a guy like Lewis Barett.

Lewis had been in Vietnam for about six weeks before he got into his first bit of trouble with the MPs. He was walking back from the Commissary in Saigon when a five ton truck assigned to the 82nd Airborne Division almost ran over him in the road. Lewis, known for him intemperate personality, picked up a big rock that was in the road and chunked it at the truck, breaking out the rear windshield. The driver immediately slammed on the brakes, put the truck in reverse and rolled back up to where Lewis was standing.

"Hey, you little turd," the driver yelled. "Are you the little bastard that knocked out my window with a rock?"

"You bet your sweet ass, asshole. Anyone who drives like you should be locked up to protect the public from being killed by a reckless driver!" Lewis screamed back at him.

The truck driver rolled out of the truck with a tire tool and came at Lewis, who calmly drew a .45 caliber pistol and said in a calm voice, "Come on, meat head. I would just as soon kill a fat pig of a truck driver as Charlie today." Needless to say, the truck driver got back into his truck and finished his trip back to the motor pool. Once there, he reported the incident, and PFC Lewis Barett was standing before SGT Major Briggs within a few hours, trying to explain why he had drawn a pistol on one of his fellow soldiers.

"Son," Briggs had said to him, "this is a very hostile country for us as Americans. We send a couple hundred people home in body bags or flag-draped coffins every week as a result of the Viet Cong or the NVA's actions in the field or because they were killed in combat in the boonies. The last thing we need is to have to send a soldier home who was killed by one of his own and try to explain to his loved ones at home how we let that happen. Am I getting through to you, son? Since this is the first time you have come before me for something like this, I am going to let this slide. Don't make me regret my decision and have to take harsher action against you the next time. Do we understand each other?"

"Do you want to hear my side of the issue?" Lewis asked Briggs.

"Son, it doesn't matter what started this whole thing. We have to work together over here to win the war. Personally, if I took my anger out every time I thought it was justified on some other US military person, I would have been busted back to a private a long time ago. If you have a legitimate complaint, then file it with the commanding officer of your unit.   Let him deal with it. Otherwise, you will lose rank and spend a lot of your time in the brig. Got it?"

"Yes, SGT Major," Lewis replied grudgingly.

Somehow, Briggs just knew that he would be seeing and hearing more about this young man in the days and weeks to come. He was not wrong. In the next five months, Lewis Barett somehow was promoted to sergeant, E-5, and still managed to get called before his commanding officer on three other occasions for petty theft, assault and battery, and intimidating another soldier in the unit.   "The kid had fire, that's for damn sure," thought Briggs. "Too bad it can't be channeled to fighting Charlie in the field!"

That was then; this is now. Now, Briggs could use the little bugger to work for him in his covert plan to continue to implement stealing weapons and selling them for his own personal gain. He would have to figure out a way to contact Barett and make him an offer he couldn't refuse. It seems that he had read in Barett's file that he was a regular at one of the massage parlors in Saigon, and if his memory served him well, it was Top of the Moon Massage Parlor in Cholon. Briggs knew that these parlors would do just about anything to get American dollars, so he knew he could probably flush the kid out by focusing on his frequent visits to the massage parlor. What Briggs would have to do would be to use a cover name and identity to contact the operator of the Top of the Moon and play it by ear from that point on. He still had some friends in the Saigon area who were flying below the radar and who were loyal to Briggs, not the US Government. He would definitely have to think all of this through before he acted on his plan, but he was sure he could pull it off.

Chapter 35

Briggs Makes a Major Miscalculation

The CIA had been scouring Briggs' every known move going back over a year to see if they could find some sort of paper trail that would lead them to his current location. Yes, Briggs was pretty damn smart, but what he forgot was that the CIA performed dark operations as an ongoing feature of their office. It might take them a while to figure things out, but they eventually would be able to pick up on something that would tie him into the security leak and the weapons for information scheme. Briggs was correct in calculating that he should flee the country, because if and when they caught him, he would face the death penalty for treason in the time of war. He could be tried summarily in Saigon, stood up before a concrete wall and executed by a firing squad, all in a matter of days. So, the CIA would go about its job of gathering the facts and then provide them to the commander of MACV and let the cards fall where they may.

Colonel Forsett called John and Klahan into his office to bring the colonel up to date on everything that was currently known or suspected about SGT Major Briggs.

"Colonel," John began, "basically, what we know is that this was a well-planned event that Briggs carried out without much help. No one saw him disappear in Bangkok, and he hasn't surfaced yet. However, the CIA is going over every trip he made while he was here, all of his contacts here and in the US, every piece of paper that he touched and everything else he did while he was assigned here. This problem didn't start immediately when he came into the command, so there had to be some catalyst to jump-start it. What we need to figure out is when this began to happen. Did this start after an R&R, a trip home on

118

leave, a traumatic event in his life or in the life of someone in his family? Something made him flip. No doubt money was involved, or why else would he risk the loss of his career, and either imprisonment or capital punishment for acts against the US Government in a war zone?

The CIA was repeating a thorough background reinvestigation on Briggs, and they would take the smallest lead and discover something that could lead to his whereabouts. What they really needed now was a break. They were about to get a lead out of nowhere that could possibly help them find the errant Daniel Briggs.

*   *   *   *   *

Briggs had contacted the operator of the Top of the Moon Massage Parlor by way of a secret letter with no forwarding address and no obvious identity of who he was or what his goal would be. He simply wanted the operator to contact him through a Lewis Barett, and Briggs was willing to pay handsomely to make that happen. In a show of good faith, Briggs had enclosed a crisp $100 bill with his letter of introduction. He had promised the operator another $400 once the parlor operator had put him in touch with Barett. He had included a description of the young man, along with a message to Barett that he thought might get him to respond, so Briggs could consider whether or not to trust his gut on including the kid in his plan to continue to steal from the US Government.

It took a while, but finally Barett came into the parlor, and the note was passed to him. Barett read the note briefly, and then again when he returned home from his partying that evening:

"Sergeant Barett, you probably will remember me when I remind you of whom I am. I was the SGT Major that you came before when you threw the rock and knocked out the window of the 82nd Airborne truck. I also know that you've had a few other skirmishes with the MPs since you left my office that day. I won't

119

belabor the issue, but I have watched your career since you have been in Vietnam, and although I am not so sure you will rise in the ranks because of your brashness and outspoken personality, I am sure that I have a job for you that would fit you perfectly.

"You may not have heard the news yet, but I have decided to leave the Army due to an opportunity to make some serious money here in Saigon, as well as other reasons that would not concern you. I am no longer living in the Saigon area, but rather I am living somewhere else in Southeast Asia, where my talents and abilities can help me profit from this crazy war. I am willing to offer you an opportunity to join me in my quest for riches and fortune, assuming your loyalty to yourself is greater than your loyalty to a government that would throw you to the dogs and then laugh at you when you fail. If you are interested, you can contact me by giving your answer back to the man who gave you this envelope, and he will see that I get it. Once you have confirmed to me that you are willing to come over to the other side, I will give you all the details that you will need to know how to contact me. Just go back to the parlor where you received this note in two weeks, and I will contact you again. I can increase your income by tenfold if you choose to work with me on this matter. Briggs."

Barett gave the note some serious consideration, and then without giving it another thought, he called the S-2 office at MACV and reported it to the Officer on Duty. Within a few hours, Barett got a call from Colonel Forsett's office telling him to report immediately and to ask for the colonel. Before the end of the day, Barett was standing before the colonel, note in hand.

"First of all, sir," Barett spoke to the colonel with confidence but in a reserved voice, "I want to say that this was a note that was presented to me just out of the blue. I have not had any prior contact with SGT Major Briggs since the dressing down he gave me that time when I retaliated against a truck driver who tried to run me off the road a few weeks after I arrived in Saigon. I also had no knowledge that he had even left the MACV office until he stated it in the note, as you can see, sir. I was going to write back to him and tell him that I was not a traitor nor a thief and no amount of money would be worth being identified as a communist sympathizer or a coward. However, I thought the best thing for me to do was to come to you and let you deal with this situation." Barett paused to get his breath and fortify himself and began speaking once more. "You see, sir, I have been in some trouble in my life. I have been in a little trouble since I've been in the Army, too, but I want to get control of that stuff because I believe I will make a good soldier and can earn the respect of my peers and my family by succeeding here. There is absolutely no way I would ever do anything as stupid as to go against my country and my fellow soldiers."

"Yes, SGT Barett, I understand your concern that we would think that you were somehow tied up with Briggs and that you had gotten cold feet and just didn't want to be involved anymore," the colonel replied. "It was an act of courage and bravery that you performed today, and we will see that you are recognized in a proper way when the time comes for those events to take place."

"So what do we do now, sir?" the young sergeant asked with some concern. "Do I just not contact him and let him go away?"

The colonel answered with a small gleam in his eye, "Oh, no, sergeant. We have a plan that I think will draw the SGT Major out, so we can locate his new base of operations. Are you up for some counter-espionage?"

"Well, sir, I took theatre and drama in my college electives, so I think I can pull it off, if that's what you want me to do."

"OK," the colonel said. "We will work out the plan on how we intend to trap him, and you will need to follow that plan to the letter. However, the first thing we need for you to do is to reply to his note and say that you aren't sure if you'd want to do it, but you are willing to listen to his plan. Once you secure that information, we will try to minimize your involvement in the rest of the take-down. So, this is what you tell him in your answer to his note."

The colonel and John crafted an answer that would not make the sergeant look too anxious or skeptical in the eyes of Briggs. They put it in the language of a young soldier who had had some issues with the law in the past, and they gave it to Barett to deliver to the man at the Top of the Moon Massage Parlor.

Chapter 36

To Catch a Traitor You Need to be Sneaky

John Bremen was to assume a new identity and pursue Briggs to the ends of the Earth, if possible, to detect whoever else was involved. Briggs would spot the name Bill Hicks almost instantaneously, so their odds of finding and catching him without a new undercover persona for John were not very good. John would become Roger Tolliver, a businessman from Idaho who worked for the State Department in weights and measures. He would be inspecting incoming and outgoing shipments for companies that did business with MACV in Vietnam. The goal was to set a trap once the weapons for shipment were identified so they could be traced to and from their source. It would not be as difficult a task as finding Briggs' actual physical location, but it would be challenging enough for John and Klahan.

John would have Barett communicate back to Briggs through the massage parlor operator, and then he would assume whatever role Barett would have taken to get a line on where Briggs was hiding. It wasn't a deep and difficult plot to follow, but one slip, and Briggs would be gone forever.

The CIA and Thailand military police had narrowed down the possible places that Briggs could have gone by sea-going vessels, and the airport surveillance did not pick up anyone who resembled Briggs boarding a flight anytime during the time period that was specified to them. There were five ships that had left Bangkok during the hours when Briggs went missing. The five destinations were Singapore, Manila, Brunei, Taipei, and Kumamoto. After extensive background research, the CIA and Thai police decided that Taipei and Kumamoto were the ones that Briggs would have fled to avoid capture by the CIA or the Thailand police. John and Klahan would need to follow up in each city to see if they could pick up his trail before he made another major arms deal. They would begin by checking with each ship's captain to determine exactly which ports the ships would have entered and see if they could get any clarification on whether or not they remembered having taken someone to one of the two ports in question during the time frame when Briggs had disappeared. What made it a little more challenging was the fact that more than one ship visited each of these ports at various times, so it would simply be a test of their patience to run down every potential lead until they found the right ship that Briggs used for his escape from Thailand.

"Klahan, I was going to suggest that we break down these various shipping companies into two lists, and we could cover twice as much ground than if we went together to do the interviews. However, I think we need to go as a team. One of us should listen, and the other one should ask the questions. You know, it's pretty hard to question someone and observe all of his reactions without having another pair of eyes and ears to look for a more hidden reason or response to certain questions. So, we go as a team and take whatever time we need to make sure we don't leave any stone of evidence uncovered."

"I think that is an excellent idea, John. We can swap off playing 'Good Cop, Bad Cop,' if that type of tactic will help us. I think it will take all of our wits to find this guy. He's not only got a head start on us, but he also had a plan going on that we aren't assured we can even detect from our investigations. This guy has been doing this type of thing for quite a while, and he is probably good at it."

"Let's try the docks where the ships leave for Singapore, first," John suggested to Klahan. "If we don't get some strong vibes from our initial interview with the Singapore leads, we can move on to the dock for Kumamoto. If we get lucky and get a lead from either of these two destinations, we will run with that lead until it no longer is viable. I believe once we get a thread of evidence that leads us one way or the other, we can begin to narrow our search."

So, without delay, they packed for their trip to Bangkok. They would fly out in the morning on a MAC flight to avoid suspicion, just in case Briggs had left someone in Bangkok to mislead anyone who might be trying to trail him.

Chapter 37

Money Greases the Wheels of Justice

Bright and early the next morning, Klahan and John bade goodbye to Tuyen and left for Tan Son Nhut and their flight to Bangkok. Tuyen had been much happier since they had learned that the people responsible for causing the deaths of their families had been killed by the Americans in the Battle for Hue. While that information would not bring back her beloved family, it did give her some closure. She had settled into her current situation in Saigon and was running a very successful business sanctioned by both the Americans and the City of Saigon Governments. There was still much to be decided about this war with the Chinese-backed North Vietnamese and the Viet Cong, but for now she had some peace of mind that she was as safe as she could be in a war-torn country such as Vietnam. She would keep the faith with Klahan and believed that each day that followed the next would be better for her and her beloved country.

*   *   *   *   *

The flight time between Saigon and Bangkok was about two hours since John and Klahan were flying in a turbo prop C-130 MAC flight, and the pilot was in no particular hurry to get there and back. After all, he was paid flight pay, hazard duty pay, and who knows what other amenities to fly them over there under the guise of another R&R trip to the lovely and sinful city of Bangkok. This trip would be anything other than fun for both of them. However, they had decided that they would exhaust every lead until they had found some way to begin tracing that cowardly and traitorous Briggs. There really was no definitive way to know

126

exactly how many military and civilian lives were directly affected by the security leak that Briggs had participated in for almost two years. It would be hard for John not to shoot the son-of-a-bitch in the head when he caught him; and, he knew he eventually would catch him.

The flight touched down at the main airport in Bangkok at 1100 hours, and John and Klahan claimed their bags and made for the exit at the front door of the terminal. They had determined to act like they were tourists, so they had booked a room at the Windsor Hotel, and they would use their hotel room as a central office as they compiled the data they would need to trace Briggs. They still wanted to keep a low profile, so they had to meet some local girls at the bar in the lobby to appear as if they were just soldiers on a leave from Vietnam. This part they didn't have any trouble with, for it came natural to them to drink and flirt with beautiful young Thai women. This part of their cover they had down pat. Unfortunately, they could not take them back to their room since the job they were doing was considered a top secret mission.

They decided to get lunch on the street in downtown Bangkok before they headed to the docks to begin their quest for Briggs. It's what most American and other Allied soldiers did when they first got to Bangkok—it was unfortunate that this would be only a shopping trip because they had no time to purchase and enjoy any of the specialties of this highly carnal city. One of the things that they were able to do was to get good directions to the docks where the trips to various destinations were booked and where, as they were told in confidence, you could get a trip "off the record" for a certain sum of American dollars. This news was promising, as they thought that Briggs might have paid top dollar to avoid ship manifests and other control factors that the local government would be able to track if they wanted to do so.

*   *   *   *   *

After visiting five different shipping offices at the docks and coming up empty in their search for leads that might help them trace Briggs, they had to sit down and rethink their approach.

"OK, John," Klahan asked his friend, "if you were looking for a ride out of this city, and you wanted it to be undetected, just how would you go about setting it up so you could pull it off?"

John thought for a minute and then said, "I think I would ask someone local who wouldn't have any particular reason to report my inquiry to the local authorities for a way to meet someone who would take money under the table to help me accomplish my task. I would only deal with cash. There could be no way to trace a cash transaction, unless someone else came along looking for me with even more cash and who could convince whoever spirited me out of the country to replicate the act. Of course, the key here would be to find the right ship captain and have enough money to offer him to convince him it would be worth his while. Since we have the full authority and backing of the US Government, cash will not be the thing that prevents us from pulling this off. We simply have to be smart enough to figure out how to find the ship captain. The rest we can handle, one way or the other."

"When in Rome, do as the Carthaginians," John said, "Rape, pillage and burn!" John had heard that saying from his Uncle Chad for years, and it meant literally what it implied. When you are in a strange place, and you have the upper hand, you do what you need to do to reach your objective. Now, they had no intention of carrying out the exact things the Carthaginians had done in Rome, but they had decided that they would use whatever force they needed to find Briggs' exit path from Thailand. "Let's get our hands a bit dirty and go grubbing with the lower class of people in this fair city," John said to Klahan.

Klahan looked at John and immediately connected with his thoughts and intentions. "I'm in, my friend," he said with a wink and a smile.

128

They decided to find some low-life rascals down at the docks to see if good old American dollars might loosen up some tongues and lead them to Briggs and his exit strategy. The first thing to do, in John's mind, was to visit some of the bars near the docks and see if anyone would identify Briggs by his picture. Of course, they needed good intelligence, so they would have to be careful how they inquired after Briggs, or they would get false information. They didn't need the barmaids and bartenders to just give them information for dollars—they needed the correct information. John would give some serious thought to the questions that he would ask to make sure that happened.

So they began their journey down the boardwalk area of the docks and stopped in on each bar and lounge as they progressed down the strip toward the ships that were moored all in a row, pointing seaward toward the mouth of the harbor. Their routine was to go to the innkeeper or owner and show Briggs' picture. If they saw any sign that he had been in the lounge, they would begin to talk about money to find out more about the conversation that might have gone on with the bar owner or cocktail waitress who had served him. So far, there was nothing but blank stares from each place they had stopped.

It was getting late in the day, and they were going to make one more call before they gave up for the day and started their search over in the morning. They decided to get a drink and end their days' search at the Pig 'N Whistle. A drop-dead gorgeous Thai cocktail waitress approached them and asked what they would like from the bar.

"Johnny Walker Black on the rocks, if you have it," John said. "Bring my friend here the same," he added.

A few minutes later, she brought the drinks and John asked, "We are looking for someone and wondered if you might have seen him?"

"Why are you looking for him?" she asked somewhat skeptically.

John's ears and senses perked up on this response from the beautiful girl, and he continued, "Well, you see, he is a buddy of ours, and we need to find him."

She looked at him with a "Sure, a buddy, huh?" Her doubt was so obvious that it made John blush for having told her the lie. So he decided to level with her. "What the hell," he thought to himself. "She probably would tell me the truth if I told her the truth." It was just a guess on his part, but he often was right about things like this.

"To be perfectly honest with you, this guy took something from us, and we are looking to get it back. I don't want to lie to you because you seem like a very nice young lady, and I don't want to disrespect you in that way," John said with true feelings of contrition from having tried to mislead her in the first place.

"Wait here," she said and disappeared. In a few minutes, a burly looking guy came out of the kitchen and said to them, "You looking for that little fat American guy who was in here a few weeks ago, huh? What's in it for me if I help you? You know there is nothing in Bangkok for free!"

"It depends on how good your information is," John said. "So, what do you know that can help us find him?"

"I know the shipmaster I sent him to. Is that good enough for you?" the manager said with a scowl. "If not, get the hell out of my bar!" He was beginning to get mad, and the color in his face began to get red as he bellowed out his threat.

"We are happy to pay you for what you know," Klahan said, taking up the conversation where John had left off just a few minutes ago. "My friend and I did not mean to insult you, but it is very important to us to find him."

"Five hundred dollars in US cash," the bartender said. "You give me $500, and I will take you to the boat and introduce you to the captain."

"OK, when do we go?" John asked.

"Now, if you have $500 in your pocket," he said.

"I'll give you $250 now and $250 when we meet the captain. Is that a deal?"

"OK," he said grudgingly, "but let me see that you have all of the money in your pocket.

John conveniently exposed his Walther PPK as he was showing the roll of $100 bills in his pocket, just in case this guy thought he might take advantage of them. "We're ready to go when you are," he said. In less than five minutes, they were out the door, heading for the docks.

"Where does this ship go?" John asked the bartender. "Do you know if he has a routine run of ports, or will he go wherever someone is willing to pay him to go?"

"That's for you to ask him," the bartender said. "I will only get you to him and introduce you to him. This is the captain that I gave the little fat guy a lead on for getting him out of the country undetected on a ship."

Klahan, John and the bartender walked a long way down the boardwalk where the boats were moored before they made a left turn onto a smaller pier that split off into a cove further down in the harbor. They walked another hundred yards or so when the bartender said, "Here it is," and he pointed to an old trawler tied up to the dock.

"Do you think this boat is sea-worthy? I don't think I would want to travel to a distant destination on a tub like that!" John exclaimed.

About that time, someone came out of the cabin area of the trawler, went into the bar and confronted them by saying, "Who said you would be invited to take a trip on my ship anyway? You must have more money than sense if you can't figure out why my ship looks the way it does. It's called being discrete, and as you said, no one would even think about going on a long trip in a tub like this one. What a person doesn't see is that under that rusty old bucket of bolts is a stainless steel hull and a two thousand diesel horse power engine and enough fuel storage to get me from Bangkok to Tokyo Harbor and halfway back to Bangkok. I'm the fastest boat in the South China Sea, with the exception of the Japanese and Chinese gun boats."

Then he asked quite calmly, "So who wants to go where and when?" He opened a beer and began to sip on it.

"Captain," John began, "we are looking for a man who very probably took your ship to some port either in Japan or Singapore, and it is very important that we locate him as soon as possible. We understand that you will want to be compensated for helping us, and I can assure you that we will pay you handsomely for your information."

"What amount of money in your mind is 'handsomely?'" the captain asked.

"It depends on what information you have to share," Klahan answered. "For a little information, we reward accordingly. However, for in depth information we will pay a lot more. Do you understand?"

"Just to let you know that I understand how the game is played, I will give you a bit of information for free. First, give me the description of this American who you are looking for."

Klahan described Briggs to the captain, observing the captain carefully.

"Yes, I did take this man to a port in the area near Japan. However, to find out more information, you will need to meet my terms. If you meet those terms, I will not only tell you where I took him, but I will take you there also for an additional fee. Do we have a deal?"

Klahan looked at John, and they both nodded to each other, and the negotiations began in earnest. "So how much money do you want for this information?"

"Five thousand dollars," he spoke without equivocation. "You give me $2,500 up front and $2,500 when I put you in at the dock where I dropped him off. Now, I can't promise you that he is still in the place where I dropped him off, but it will definitely give you a jump start on finding him. What do you say? Have we got a deal?"

"Let me confer with my partner for a minute, Captain. I'm sure we can work this out to our mutual satisfaction," John replied.

John pulled Klahan aside to discuss the proposition that the captain had made to them. While the amount of money he was asking for did not bother him, he wanted to make sure that the captain was not playing both ends against the middle.

"Knowing Briggs, I imagine the last thing he would have done is let this captain lead anyone back to him, so we are probably safe assuming that Briggs left the port and moved on somewhere else in country or to some remote area of the island chain," Klahan said. "I believe this is a good opportunity to pick up Briggs' trail, and we can get the CIA to trace his movements from the port to the area around the general port area and see if we can get a break on his whereabouts."

"I agree with you, Klahan," John echoed. "Let's see if we can get some more info on Briggs from the captain. He probably knows some stuff that will help us, even if he doesn't know he possesses that info."

"Captain," John began, "did you happen to write this guy's name down in your log?"

"Of course," the captain said. "We are required by the government to keep a record of all people traveling on our vessels in and out of Thailand. If my memory serves me well, I doubt the name or papers he showed me were legitimate, though. He just seemed a little jumpy and suspicious to me."

"We just need the information for our report." John was thinking all the while that Briggs probably thought that this new identity that he was probably using to escape from Bangkok would never be called into question. Actually, that's how they would track him to his new location—not from his real identity, but rather from his new one.

"What did he say his name was?" John asked the bartender.

"Let me look it up," the captain said. "Joseph Moreno," he said. "He showed me his passport and driver's license."

John flashed a picture of Briggs to the captain.

"Yep. That's the little bastard. He had shifty eyes, and I figured he was up to no good, but I had no idea he was in trouble with his government. I just took his money and deposited him on an island with a harbor. What did the little bugger do to get a manhunt after him, anyway?"

"It's complicated," John replied. "But if you can get us to the same harbor without delay, I will double your monetary request. Time is of the essence with this guy."

"How soon can you leave?" the captain asked.

"Now would be fine with me and Klahan, if you are prepared to go," John said. "I just need to get my luggage from the car."

The captain called over one of the bar girls and spoke quietly to her. Then, without hesitation he set out for the captain's deck on the ship to get them underway. John and Klahan threw their duffle bags onboard, and the mission to find and neutralize Briggs was in high gear.

PART III: A MOVING TARGET

Chapter 38

I am Alive and Living in Japan

Jimmy Garrison was beginning to think that his Cousin Danny must be missing in action or that something else really bad had happened to him since it had been several weeks since Jimmy had heard from him, and the time for a routine shipment of AK-47s was coming up. Jimmy really had no way to contact Briggs. Briggs had always made the effort to contact Jimmy since there were times when Briggs simply couldn't contact Jimmy for weeks at a time due to the nature of his work with the MACV in Saigon. However, this was the longest stretch of time that they had not communicated since they had started their smuggling operation.

Surely, as Jimmy pondered the length of delay in speaking to Danny, there was a good reason for it. He would just have to sit tight and see what happened. It was Jimmy's bosses who worried him. They were less forgiving once they had been promised guns or money, and they tended to take it out on lower ranking soldiers like Jimmy. Jimmy had not made his bones totally, and this delay in weapons delivery was not helping his situation at all. It was time for his cousin to show up!

*   *   *   *   *

Briggs had been getting his sources lined up to resume the shipment of AK-47s through a connection that he had established in Saigon before he had left for Kumamoto. For some reason, Lewis did not take the bait. That was OK with him, as he always thought the kid was a little unstable, and the odds of the kid finding him and exposing him were slim. What Briggs did not want to do was to lose his connection with the mafia chiefs whom he and Jimmy had groomed for this project over a period of almost two years.

Monday morning Jimmy got an unexpected telephone call.

"Will you accept a collect call from a Danny Briggs?" the operator said when he picked up the telephone.

"Sure," he said gratefully now that Briggs had finally contacted him.

"Jimmy, how in the hell are you, my boy?" Briggs asked as if nothing unusual had happened the last few weeks.

"I'm fine, Danny. I was beginning to worry a little about you, cousin. Is everything going well over there?"

"We've had a little complication that I don't want to discuss over the telephone, but I have bought you an airplane ticket to Tokyo for this Saturday, and I want you to meet me at the Imperial Hotel in the Ginza area of Tokyo. I will leave further instructions for you at the desk in your name. Can you make it?"

"Yeah, I'll be there. Anything else I should know before I come to see you? Are we going to have any supply issues with our current deal? I'm getting a lot of pressure on my end, and it would be good to be able to tell my partners what's going on."

"I really can't say over the telephone, but it will be well worth your time to make the trip. "

"OK, see you Saturday," Jimmy answered and hung up the telephone less than satisfied with Cousin Danny's answers.

*   *   *   *   *

Five days and six-thousand nautical miles later, Jimmy was standing in the lobby of the Imperial Hotel in Tokyo. "This is one fabulous hotel," he thought to himself. His instructions at the front desk were to have a seat in the lobby and wait for Cousin Danny to find him.

"How was the trip?" Jimmy heard a familiar voice from behind his back. "Don't turn around, but go back to the front desk and get a key for the fifteenth floor suite that I have reserved in your name. It is prepaid, so all you need to do is show them your passport, and they will give you the key. Take the elevator, let yourself in the room, and I will join you in a few minutes."

"May I help you with your luggage, sir," the bellman asked Jimmy as he boarded the elevator.

"No need," he said. "It's lightweight, and I only have one bag. Here's a tip for your courtesy in asking me, anyway." The last thing he needed was to show up in the room and have Cousin Danny walk in on him and a stranger.

The bellman made a small bow to Jimmy and pushed the fifteenth floor button for him before stepping off the elevator.

"Jimmy!" Danny exclaimed as he came into the room and gave his cousin a big bear hug. "How the hell are you? Was the trip OK on the way over?"

Jimmy looked a bit skeptical at Briggs and said, "Cuz, I think you've got a bit of explaining to do. The family back home is getting a little anxious about getting the supply of AK-47s, and we are running about a month behind in the distribution of them back in Texas. Can you fill me in on what's happening here?"

"Not to worry, Jimmy, as I have things under control. However, I have lost my first contact with the suppliers due to an investigation that's going on over there. I had to leave the country in the dead of night to avoid being implicated in espionage and gun running over there. I think I have figured out how to get reconnected with the supplier of the AK-47s, and I should have some on the way soon."

"Danny, the family doesn't like disappointments like these. I will get you a little more time, but these guys do not understand if their schedule has to be altered for any reason. Do you get my drift?"

"Yeah, I got it," Briggs answered with little to no emotion in his voice. "However, I believe that I am the only game in town when it comes to these types of weapons. You should remind your family members that this is not something just anyone can supply them—at any cost."

"Fine, but let's come up with a story I can take back to Dallas that will buy us a little time." And with that comment, Cousin Jimmy was headed back to the airport.

Chapter 39

A Boat Ride to Kumamoto

"Hey, John," Klahan said when he looked up from his book that he had been reading for the past three days on board the ship, "do you think this tub is ever going to get us to Japan in our lifetimes?"

"Patience, Klahan. I thought you Asians were into all of the mind-altering self-discipline of Kung Fu, Jiu Jitsu, and Taoism to teach yourselves to have a calming effect on all those people and things around you. If so, you just failed the test." John waited with anticipation for Klahan's response.

"Hey, dude," he said with great pride, "I'm a twentieth-century man. I can't be bothered with all of that mysticism and spooky spiritualism that they teach. It's not practical in the age of jet planes and trips to outer space!"

"The captain said it would take about four days to get to Kumamoto, and we are just completing day three. I imagine that we will get there sometime tomorrow. One thing I do know is that we should have an airtight plan in place to hunt down Briggs. He probably thinks that he is safe, and that no one will be able to find him in Japan. It will be a great day when we burst that bubble of his. With our ability to track people all over the world with the CIA and their surveillance programs, no one can hide indefinitely."

"OK," Klahan asked, "what was the alias that he used to help him escape from Bangkok? Jerry Romano? No, it was Joseph Romano."

"So, we get the CIA to begin searching all transactions in the name of Joseph Romano in and around Kumamoto, Japan. If he has bought a car, rented a hotel room or opened a bank account in that name, we will narrow our search for him and eventually catch the bastard."

"It's only been a little more than twenty years since V-J Day, and I'm not so sure how much cooperation we will get from the local police, John. Have you given any thought to that possible problem?"

"I have it on good authority that the local law enforcement people will be happy to help us catch a criminal hiding in their country. The last thing that Japan needs is an international incident where they can be blamed for harboring a traitor from the US Army. If for no other reason than that they will not want a stigma added to the ones that have lingered since the war, they will want to help us. This is where you can really help us because you know more of the customs of Asia than I do."

"True," Klahan said, "but the Japanese are about as different from the Vietnamese as the British are from you Yanks! But, I will do what I can to bridge the gap with them when we try to explain why we are on an unauthorized mission to find and either kidnap or eliminate someone who has chosen to take refuge within their sovereign borders."

"When you put it like that, I see how that could present a problem. As far as I am concerned, we can just eliminate the bastard. That will stop the gun running issues and probably help eliminate the information leak as well. Unfortunately, our orders are to find Briggs and take him back to MACV Headquarters alive."

"I'm not promising anything to anyone, with the exception that we will fix this leak—one way or the other," Klahan said.

"Let's get some shut-eye now and do some serious planning on capturing Briggs tomorrow morning after breakfast."

Chapter 40

A Quick Trip to Seoul

Briggs had heard that there was some sympathy in Seoul, South Korea, for the NVA and Viet Cong among some of the people in the city. He had a lead on a former North Korean soldier who held such an opinion. This was going to be tricky, but not an impossible task. Money, especially American dollars, was always a great medium. He landed at Jeju International Airport and took the train from there to Seoul. He arranged to meet Samir Lee Kim at Seobook Myeonok for lunch.

"Are you Joseph Romano?" the very polite Korean young man asked of Briggs as he walked into the restaurant. His mastery of the English language wasn't perfect, but it was pretty damn good.

"Yes, and you must be Samir?" Briggs answered.

With a small bow of his head, Samir said, "Yes. I am Samir, and I think I can help you with your problem in Saigon. I have family members who have fled from the north to the south in Vietnam, and they are very familiar with the problems that exist over there."

"Let's get a table in the back of the restaurant so we can speak freely," Briggs said and motioned to the waiter to seat them in a booth in the rear of the restaurant.

Once seated, Briggs said to Samir, "Look, I am trying to open a sort of trade route in Vietnam that is not exactly approved by the governments of either the United States or Vietnam. Hell, I don't imagine the government of South Korea would approve either. What I need is for someone to work with the mercenaries who can trade me AK-47s for information on the troop movements of the ARVN and American forces in the field. Is that something your people can help me pull off in Vietnam?"

"What is in it for them, besides getting back at the US and the ARVN troops for killing their friends and families with their napalm and B-52 bombers?"

"I can guarantee American dollars for any help they give us in getting our shipments in and out of Saigon and on to the United States. The amount of money they will receive will be based on the number of AK-47s they are able to help us move out of the country."

"I see," Samir said with an understanding look on his face. "Do you know how many of these AK-47 rifles you want to ship to the US?"

"I would like to ship one thousand a month to Dallas, Texas, and I have lost my connection with the shipping company that I used in the past. I would need some help identifying another source of transportation to make sure they arrived in Dallas in a timely manner. Can you help there, too?"

"Mr. Romano, anything can be accomplished with enough American dollars paving the way for that success," Samir said with a slight grin. "We just need to work out the details. Give me a telephone number where I can reach you, and I will call you when I have an answer for you."

"I will call you, Samir, in about a week to see if you have come up with a solution to my problem. Otherwise, I will have to seek help from some other source," Briggs bluffed as he stood up and ended the conversation with Samir.

"OK, Mr. Romano. Here is my business card. If I do not answer the telephone when you call me, please leave a message on how I can return the call and share what I know at that time."

Both men shook hands, and they left the restaurant on their way to their home destinations.

Briggs was not totally sure about Samir, but it was his best bet at this time, and it gave him something legitimate to tell Cousin Jimmy when he contacted Briggs for an update. And, Briggs knew, Jimmy would be contacting him soon.

Briggs boarded his flight to Kumamoto and felt pretty good about things. He had more than $500,000 in an offshore bank account, and so far he had evaded any suspicion of his involvement in the affairs of Saigon and the weapons for information inquiry.

"A cold, tall beer, and I will be happy when I land in Kumamoto."

Chapter 41

A Big Needle in a Small Haystack

John and Klahan landed at the dock in Kumamoto and took a taxi into town to find a room for the night. They stayed at an inexpensive inn and formulated their plan for the next few days over a bottle of Johnny Walker Black that John had stowed in his duffle bag.

"So, where do you think we should start, John? This guy could be almost anywhere, and there are about ten million people in this area. What do you think our odds are of finding and bringing the son-of-a-bitch back to Saigon?"

"Well, Klahan, although it's like finding a needle in a haystack, this haystack is small and the needle is big!" he said with a smile.

"I just don't get that needle and haystack stuff, but I'll take your word for it. How do we narrow the field so we are not running all over town trying to locate this guy? And by the way, he will probably be looking for someone like us to be after him, don't you guess?"

"All of that is true, Klahan. However, we have a secret weapon. The CIA has been following all the leads tied to his new identity since we left Saigon four days ago. We will touch base with them as our first stop and see if they can shed any light on where Briggs has decided to live and rekindle his weapons for intelligence plan. The good news for us is that Briggs thinks we are trying to find him from his old identification papers. That should help us find him a lot faster because I doubt that he has changed his identity again so soon."

"It seems you are in search of your own identity, John. First you're John Bremen, then you're Bill Hicks, then you're John Bremen again, and now you're Bill Hicks again. It's enough to boggle the mind!"

John couldn't help but laugh at Klahan's comment. He was right, though. If John wasn't careful, he might confuse himself with whoever he was supposed to be at any particular time.

"Yep," John said and looked at Klahan with a bit of a smirk, "I think I might have an identity crisis." John and Klahan broke out into laughter, which they both needed right now.

Chapter 42

Dallas is a Civilized City

Jimmy "The Hammer" Garrison was born in Dallas, Texas, and attended a good Catholic high school in the suburbs. His ancestors hailed from Sicily—Corleone to be exact—and that was a necessary element to having the opportunity to achieve the level of Don in any US crime family. His credentials were as good as gold.

Although he wasn't an outstanding student, he managed to finish high school with a GED diploma and immediately went down to the US Army recruiting office to sign up for Vietnam.

"You have flat feet, Garrison," the Army doctor told him and immediately wrote "4F" on his folder. "There's no way you're going to serve in the US Army or any other military branch of the US Government with those flat feet. You couldn't hold up on a forced march or even be able to stand for long periods of time on guard duty. Looks like you lucked out, son. There'll be no Vietnam duty for you!"

"But I want to join and serve. Isn't there some way we can get around those regulations, sir?" Jimmy asked in a pleading voice.

"I'm afraid not, son. It's just a bad break for someone like you who wants to serve his country."

Actually, Jimmy wasn't that keen on getting shot at in Vietnam, but he would love to have an AK-47 or an M-16 assault rifle. That would make him 'King of the Mountain" back home in Dallas after the war ended. Jimmy had grown up hard and had moved from North Dallas with his family to East Dallas in a somewhat lawless neighborhood. He had gotten in a fight with another boy and damn near beat the boy to death. Granted, as the Dallas Police Department agreed, the other kid started it. However, Jimmy not only stopped it, he also almost stopped the other kid from breathing. The Catholic school recommended to his family that Jimmy would be better off in a public school district and suspended him indefinitely from St. Thomas Catholic High School. Although he tried to fit into some of the public schools in East Dallas, he just managed to finish his education with a GED.

"That sucks!" Jimmy said to the doctor and stormed out of the recruiting station. "If I can't join the US Army, I will join the Savoca crime family army," he mumbled to himself. "Either way, I will make some noise with some guns!"

*   *   *   *   *

It only took about three days for Jimmy to get hooked up with one of the street gangs and was well on his way to being a wanksta. He had no intention of staying tight with these common street hoodlums, but he thought it might lead him to a real mafia family and that was his new goal in life. He wanted eventually to be a Don, and he had the Italian roots to qualify, once he was a made man in the organization.

After a few months on the street, he met a man named Joey the Knife. Joey was a captain in the local mafia family in Dallas, and something about this young man caught the mobster's eye.

"Hey, kid," Joey said, "you a bad ass or what?" He teased Jimmy a bit when he saw him hanging out on a street corner in Southeast Dallas.

"What's it to you, old man?" Jimmy quipped back to the stranger who had called him out and tried to embarrass him in front of his friends.

"Well, I hear on the street that you want to meet someone in the Savoca Family. That's me, kid, if you're interested."

"Sure," Jimmy said, "let's talk." And they drove away together in the mobster's shiny new Cadillac. That was three years ago, and a lot of stuff had happened to put Jimmy on a course for big recognition by the Dallas mob family.

It took Jimmy three years to reach the level of captain in the Savoca family, and he was close to being a made man, like his Uncle Salvatore Antillo, who was the Don in Dallas when Jimmy was growing up. It was a little strange that he was following in his uncle's footsteps, although his uncle had served five to ten in Folsom Prison on racketeering charges. This AK-47 rifle deal could tip the scales in his favor and seal the deal for him, so he was doing all he could to make it happen in such a way that he alone would be credited with bringing in the guns for distribution.

Now it was up to him, and he alone could finish this deal. He would work with his cousin Danny, or he would remove Danny from the picture and make it happen by himself. Either way, this deal was his way to the top, and he wasn't going to blow it now.

Chapter 43

Tracing a Traitor

John and Klahan were ready to pursue Briggs early the next morning after their arrival in Kumamoto the day before.

"The first thing we need to do is contact the CIA office here in Japan and see what they have found for us. Since the Japanese are still sensitive about foreign soldiers residing on their soil after WWII, we will need to be cautious and try to not stir up too much public interest in this situation. The general population still looks on our country and our military with suspicion, and we need continue helping open doors, not closing them," John expressed his concerns to Klahan quietly while they were enjoying a Western-style breakfast at the open market near the Ginza.

"I agree, my friend. However, we do need to poke around enough to get some good leads on where Briggs has moved his operation. We need to apprehend him and take him back to Saigon as soon as practically possible. As long as he is free to move around and negotiate with the mercenaries in Vietnam, the more damage he can do to the US national security and add to the loss of life with the American soldiers in the field."

"I got a cable at the hotel from Colonel Forsett this morning with our contact name in Tokyo. He can put us in touch with local help who will root out Briggs and make him easier to find and capture. I had sent the colonel our location when we checked into the hotel yesterday and asked for any information that he might have that could help us move this search forward in a meaningful way. The contact's name is Michio Osamu Higashi, and I have a telephone number where we can speak to him privately and see what he has discovered over these past few days."

John called Michio's telephone number, and a soft-spoken female voice answered in broken English, "Yes, how may I help you?"

"My name is Bill Hicks, and I need to speak to Michio at his earliest convenience. Is he available to come to the telephone?"

"Yes, please. I will get him for you."

"This is Michio," a strong, well-spoken English-speaking voice replied. "Is this Bill Hicks?"

"Yes, did Colonel Forsett tell you that I would be contacting you today?" John continued and wondered just how much the colonel had shared with this CIA operative. The mission that he and Klahan were presently pursuing was not authorized or sanctioned by MACV or Washington, as far as they knew.

"He told me that you would be calling me and asking for some help. So, how can I help you, Bill Hicks?"

"Are you in Tokyo, or are you in Kumamoto?"

"I am in Tokyo, but I can be in Kumamoto tomorrow morning if it will help you with your mission. Where are you staying?"

"We are staying in a small hotel on the outskirts of Kumamoto. What I would prefer to do is to meet you somewhere in the market-place near the Ginza in Tokyo. Is that possible?"

"Oh, yes," he replied very politely. "Let's meet at Two Dragons Restaurant just off the Ginza. It is around the corner from Mitsukoshi, the oldest department store in Japan. Every taxi driver in Japan can get you to Mitsukoshi. You can walk to the restaurant from there. In fact, it would be best if you walked through the department store, as if you were there for shopping, and then exit the north side of the store, and you will see Two Dragons across the street. Say, two o'clock P.M.?"

"We will be there tomorrow. Thanks, and please bring any information with you when you come that you think might interest us."

John looked at Klahan when he finished with the telephone call and said, "I know that the old man set this thing up for us with Michio, but I don't think we should take any chances with the

151

local folk until we check the situation out and are satisfied that they are truly working to help us and not delay us."

"You are a suspicious man, John. But I agree with the motto 'Better safe than sorry' when it comes to foreign intelligence people. It's not that I don't trust the locals or the colonel, but it's our butts on the line over here, so let's do it our way!"

"Let's get some sleep and fly over in the morning. We can leave here around 9:00 AM and still arrive in plenty of time to meet Michio by 2:00 PM. It will give us some time to check out the meeting spot to make sure we are comfortable with it. Oh, by the way, please remember that I am Bill Hicks. Since Klahan is a common Vietnamese name, no one should be suspicious if your name is discovered in the aftermath of our visit."

"I've got it, Bill," Klahan said with a smile, and they gave each other the thumbs up signal.

Chapter 44

The Tokyo CIA

"Now that's what I call a department store," Klahan said as they approached Mitsukoshi. The larger than life store took up a city block and was lit up like a Christmas tree.

"Macy's in New York hasn't got anything on Mitsukoshi's here in Tokyo," John said with wonder. "This place is like Disneyland and NASA rolled into one gigantic space."

"I read it is the largest department store in the world."

"I wouldn't doubt it, now that I've seen it first hand," John said while looking at the store with childlike wonder. "I do think once we have wandered into that mammoth building, no one will be the wiser when we slip out the back door. This Michio seems to be at the top of his game."

Without another word from either of them, they slipped into the magical world of Japanese extravagance.

"There's the door on the north side of the store," Klahan said as he moved toward it with stealth and determination.

As they departed the store, John looked back momentarily, as if he really didn't want to leave this wonderland of retail. He had seen some big, beautiful department stores in America, but nothing rivaled Mitsukoshi on the Ginza—nothing at all!

They entered the Two Dragons Restaurant and immediately noticed that the level of lighting in the dining room was very dim, which made it difficult to see the tables and chairs, much less the people sitting at them.

"May I help you?" a beautiful, china doll dressed waitress asked them as they approached the maître d' stand at the front of the restaurant. She was dressed in a stunning red kimono with matching red thong slippers and had her hair up in a bun on top of her head. The pancake makeup on her face made her look like some type of movie star to John, who just stared at her unbelievable face.

Klahan answered for both of them and said, "Yes, we are meeting a gentleman named Michio here for lunch, and we wondered if he had reserved a table for us in advance?"

She looked at the reservation book and said, "Oh, yes. He is waiting for you at table eighteen in the back of the restaurant. Please follow me, and I will take you to his table."

As they were walking to the table, John whispered to Klahan in a small voice so the hostess could not hear him, "She is about the prettiest thing I have seen since I left the States."

"I noticed that you lost your ability to speak there for a few moments, my friend. But not to worry, I always have your back!" Klahan winked at John as they approached table eighteen.

As they approached the table, a young, handsome Japanese national stood up, stuck out his hand and said, "Welcome to Tokyo, Gentlemen. My name is Michio Osamu Higashi, but you can just call me Michio," and he gave them a small bow, as was the custom in Japan.

"Bill Hicks and Klahan," he said reassuringly to the CIA agent. There seemed to be an unanswered question on John's mind, but he wasn't going to ask it here.

A very large smile began to spread over Michio's face. "You didn't pick up on the fact that I was a Japanese national on the telephone, did you? Well, I was educated at Cornell University in America, and I speak English with absolutely no Asian accent."

"Yeah, I noticed," John said a little sheepishly. "I don't know what I was expecting, but it probably wasn't you. Cornell appears to have been a good choice for you. Your English is better than mine and all of my friends!" He laughed goodheartedly, and the atmosphere was suddenly warm and friendly with the three men.

"So, Michio, what have you found out that might help us find SGT Major Briggs, or Joseph Romano as he goes by these days?"

"Your SGT Major Briggs, AKA Joseph Romano, arrived in the port city of Kumamoto about three months ago, supposedly from a trip abroad. It appears that Mr. Romano had already purchased a home in the foothills of the mountains just to the north of Kumamoto and had pretty much established himself as a retired military man who was just looking to find a peaceful and quiet place to retire in solitude. We have searched for bank records and every informational and historical fact of Joseph Romano, and it appears that he didn't exist until about six months ago. I contacted Langley, and they agree that there's something not quite right about this guy. We can't place our finger on the specifics of what smells wrong about his past--that is, what past we can find in any records here or abroad, but something just doesn't add up. We have had him under surveillance for about forty-eight hours, and we have some good photos of him. Do you have a photo of this Briggs that he may be impersonating?"

In an answer to Michio, John showed him a picture of Briggs. "Does this guy look anything like your Joseph Moreno?"

"He's a dead ringer for Briggs. Well, I'll be damned. What I want to know is how the hell he slipped into Japan without anyone recognizing him or questioning his papers."

"Trust me, Michio, this guy is a pro. He served as the top enlisted man in the entire Vietnam command in an intelligence capacity. The only way that we will catch him, and the only reason that we even have a lead on him, is that he made one small mistake. He won't make many more, so we need to catch him before he disappears again into thin air."

"I have a local address for him, and we can stake out his house if you want us to and keep him under surveillance."

"He's trained to spot such tactics, so we probably should just keep an eye on him from a distance and not change the landscape, or he might get wind of it and be gone."

"Whatever you wish," Michio said in a calm and pleasant voice. "Just tell us how we can help you, and we will make it happen. We have some local policemen who will also help, if called upon, and our relationship with the government of Japan is getting better each and every day."

155

"Thanks for the offer. I think we will want to just watch him and tap his phone, if you are able to do that for us. We don't want to make our move too quickly and lose the other party in Vietnam who he is conspiring with on these things."

"We will do as you wish, Bill. Just call us anytime, and we will try to make things available to you." And with that comment, Michio was away from the table and had disappeared into thin air.

"Damn," Klahan, "how did he do that?" And they laughed all the way through their delicious lunch of noodles and sushi.

Chapter 45

The Senator's Hands Are Not Clean

Jimmy Garrison was on the hook with his Dallas mob associates to keep supplying the AK-47s, or their equivalents, to the mafia. He had established himself as a reliable and trustworthy captain in the Savoca family, and he needed this gun deal to continue uninterrupted. Danny had given him a telephone number to call when he was in Tokyo the last time they talked, and now was as good a time as ever to see if Cousin Danny had worked out the details to renew the shipments to the Dallas crime family.

Briggs' potential connection to the AK-47 rifle supply in Saigon was a problem. Samir, who Briggs had hoped would reconnect with the mercenaries in Vietnam, never reported back to him. As far as Briggs knew, Samir could be dead or missing in action. Either way, Briggs had to find another route to supplying the illicit weapons to the Dallas crime family.

"Hey, Danny," Jimmy had said when Briggs had picked up the telephone at his hideout in Kumamoto. "How's our deal going over there? Are you about ready to ship some more of those AK-47s to us? I'm getting a little heat from the family here, and I need to tell them something real soon."

"There's some good news, and there's some bad news. The bad news is that my connection with the AK-47s seems to have been interrupted by the authorities, and we will not be able to continue to ship them to you from Saigon. The good news is that I have a source in the Pentagon that can get you M-16 assault rifles instead. The beauty of that deal is that they are manufactured in the USA, and we will get them before they make their way across the Pacific Ocean to Vietnam. I can't give you the name of the source in the Pentagon, but let's just say he is a major player in politics and a power broker when it comes to military hardware. As soon as I have the details, I will call you and we can talk."

"That sounds great, Danny. Can you give me an estimated time that I can expect the first shipment so I can tell my people here in Dallas?"

"Not just yet, but I should have that info soon. I will call you as soon as I have any concrete information that you can act upon. These rifles will cost a little more, but we really don't have a choice."

When Briggs hung up, he placed an overseas call to Senator Carlos Carlson of Maryland. A young female voice answered. "Senator Carlson's Office, how may I help you?" she cooed into the telephone.

"I need to speak to the senator at once," Briggs demanded.

"I'm sorry, sir, but he is in a meeting and can't be disturbed. Can you give him a message from me?"

"You tell him that his favorite sergeant from Vietnam needs to speak to him as soon as possible. Please tell him that I will call back in about thirty minutes, and I expect for him to pick up the telephone at that time."

"Well," she continued with her standard response on calls to the senator's office, "I can't promise you that he will be available, but I will give him your message."

"Oh, I imagine he will be available for me, dear," Briggs answered her with a little sarcasm in his voice. "You just make sure he gets the message."

"Of course, Sergeant, I will get the message to him now," she said and quickly hung up.

"That son-of-a-bitch had better pick up the telephone when I call back," Briggs thought to himself. He had been paying the senator money to run interference for him for over two years, so there wasn't much chance that Senator Carlos Carlson wouldn't take his call.

"This is Senator Carlos Carlson's Office, and how may I help you today?" the now familiar voice on the other end of the telephone line answered when Briggs redialed the telephone number thirty minutes later.

"I need to speak to Senator Carlson. This is his favorite sergeant calling," he stated once again to the telephone screener.

"Oh, yes, sir. The senator has been waiting for your call. I will connect you now," and there was some clicking on the line before Carlos picked up the telephone.

"To what do I owe the pleasure of this call today, Sergeant?" the senator blustered to Briggs. "And how can I help you, my good man?"

"We need to speak about some things, and not over the telephone. I need for you to come to Tokyo and visit with me tomorrow. I will make you an airline reservation, and you need to be on that airplane without delay!" Briggs spoke with authority to this senior senator.

"Now just a minute here, son, I can't just drop everything and get on an airplane and fly half-way around the world for a lunch appointment." He laughed half-heartedly.

"You not only can do it, you will do it, Senator. I will expect you at the Two Dragons Restaurant in Tokyo at 1:00 PM tomorrow. I will send directions to you when I wire your ticket. It will be in your best interest to be on that airplane tomorrow, if you know what I mean."

"OK. I will be there, but this had better be good. I will be making a real sacrifice for my constituents to be out of Washington during a crucial vote on a budget spending bill."

"Just be there, Senator. I will explain what I will need from you once you arrive here tomorrow. It is important that you disguise this trip as something other than meeting me. I'm sure you have ways of doing that, don't you, Senator?" Briggs hung up the telephone, letting the senator fume a little by being ordered around by a lowly NCO in the US Army.

Briggs was pleased with himself knowing that he probably had the weapons smuggling issue back under control, and he always felt good when he could order some big shot from Washington around.

Chapter 46

Tightening the Noose

John and Klahan now had some credible, hard evidence on where Briggs might be hiding from the authorities. All they had to do was observe the small bungalow that Michio had indicated was his current residence and move in when they felt that it was the best time.

"They sure don't expect Americans to ride in these little cracker-box cars!" John was complaining to Klahan as they were in a stakeout within binocular distance of Briggs' house in Kumamoto.

"Well, since you are five-feet-eleven inches tall and the average Japanese man is only five-feet-four inches tall, I can see your point. It would be more obvious if we were sitting in a Crown Vic, don't you think?" Klahan was ribbing John about his complaints.

"OK, I get it. It's just not normal to have one's ears between ones knees when sitting in an automobile."

Klahan pointed to the front of the bungalow and said, "Isn't that our wayward SGT Major going into the house now?"

"Looks like it to me, but let's give him a few minutes and see if he does something stupid that we can use before we move in on him. Did the local CIA people bug his telephone, as we requested?"

"Yes, and I have a speaker keyed up for us to hear his conversations, should he be stupid enough to make important calls from that phone in his house."

Just then, they heard the telephone ringing in Briggs' house. Briggs picked it up, and they listened in.

"I will expect you at the Two Dragons Restaurant in Tokyo at 1:00 PM tomorrow. I will send directions to you when I wire your ticket. It will be in your best interest to be on that airplane tomorrow, if you know what I mean."

"OK. I will be there, but this had better be good."

They recognized Briggs' voice as the first speaker, but they weren't exactly sure who the second speaker was, but the voice seemed familiar to both of them. They tried to recall who it might have been, but it was no use. They would just have to decide if they would lay a trap for Briggs or arrest him now and let the chips fall where they may.

"This is too important to shut down the investigation at this point just because we can bag Briggs. The other voice on the telephone could be an insignificant person, or it could be the person who makes all of the final decisions for this caper. Let's go back to the Two Dragons Restaurant and check it out tomorrow and decide then if we need to close the SGT Major down now or just give him more rope to hang himself."

"Sounds good to me, and I plan to eat all of my noodles this time!" Klahan said.

They decided to check in with Colonel Forsett's office, so John got him on the telephone to bring him up to date on the news of their success of finding Briggs.

"Colonel," John said as he spoke to the commander of the MACV compound, "we have located Briggs, and we have him under surveillance."

"So, you are going to bring him in, right?" the colonel asked, seeming a little confused by John's previous statement.

"Well, about that, sir. This is our current thinking. Sure, we can put Briggs in handcuffs and bring him back to Saigon to stand court-martial for treason; or, we can let him operate a while under our surveillance and trace some of his sources to try to put an end to this matter altogether. In fact, we were able to get the local CIA boys to tap into his telephone line, and we heard a call today about a clandestine meeting in Tokyo tomorrow with one of his operatives or suppliers. We planned to go along and check it out before we shut him down. What do you think we should do, sir?"

"I like your plan, John. Just don't let that son-of-a-bitch give you the slip and disappear again."

"Well, he's pretty slick, sir. We can't promise that we won't lose him again, but we really think this whole weapons for information operations goes a lot deeper than we first thought. We think we should let it unwind a little before we slam the door shut on whoever we identify as being involved."

"Just keep me posted on your progress."

"We will, sir."

Chapter 47

The Senator and the Traitor

John and Klahan were sitting outside of the Two Dragons Restaurant in Tokyo the next day, waiting to see who would show up to speak to Briggs. They had been there for thirty minutes when a large man showed up at 12:45 PM and went inside to meet his party. There was no way of knowing if this was the man who Briggs had planned to meet or not. What they needed to do was see if Briggs showed up, and if he solicited this stranger to come out and meet him.

"Klahan, did that big guy look familiar to you just now?"

"Now that you mention it, he does look a little like that blowhard senator who came into Colonel Forsett's office a few months ago. What I remember about that incident is that it really pissed off the colonel to the point that I thought he might take out his side arm and plug the arrogant bastard!" John chuckled to himself.

"Now why do you think that this guy is connected with Briggs? As far as I can see, he may be going in there just to have lunch with him."

"Boy, Klahan, you are naïve if you think this could be a coincidence five thousand miles from California. Let's assume that he is just another link in the chain of evidence that leads us back to Briggs. I think he is nervous, and he thinks we are on to him. And he's correct because we are on to him!"

Just then, Briggs showed up and went inside.

"So what do we do now, John? Should we arrest them both?"

"There's a problem here," John told him with a troubled look on his face. "In the US, you cannot arrest a sitting senator without due cause, and we sure as hell don't have evidence of that with us. We will have to play it by ear, and if we arrest Briggs and not arrest the senator, we will blow our cover and they will go underground. That will be the last we will probably see of them, and we definitely will lose the lead on who's compromising our movements in Vietnam. No, we have to play this cool and let it develop. We will have to get the NSA, the FBI and the CIA all involved in tracing these guys. Right now, the ball is in our court, and we don't want to muck this thing up and let them off the hook. I will take a picture of the man who went in to meet Briggs and show it to the colonel once I get it developed back in Saigon. He will love it if he can stick it to that snotty bastard that dressed him down a few months ago. Hell, Klahan, this is better than a soap opera on television."

"What's a soap opera?" Klahan asked with a puzzled look on his face.

"Don't ask, and I won't have to lie to you!" John laughed as he brought his camera with the long-range lens up to take a picture of the two men as they were leaving the restaurant.

"I'll tell you one damn thing, John. You Americans sure have some funny expressions; needles in haystacks, soap operas—it's enough to make your head swim!"

John almost burst a vein in his head, he was laughing so hard. John was thinking to himself that it was probably a good thing that Klahan would never know some of those things about America. He definitely would have issues with the gangs, mob families, easy marriages and divorces—yes, Klahan would be blessed to not have to learn of those darker aspects of America.

"Let's get a good night's rest and get back to Saigon tomorrow. I want to share all of this with the colonel as soon as possible so we have a good chance of catching these guys in the act of theft and treason. I would love to see both of those bastards swinging from a rope!"

Chapter 48

How to Catch a Thief

"How was your trip back from Japan, men?" Colonel Forsett asked them when they came into his office to report in on their surveillance trip to Kumamoto.

Klahan was the first to speak up and said, "You know, Colonel, it was really difficult to let that bastard Briggs continue on his merry way once we located him and had him in our sights."

"As you can tell, sir, Klahan was for either handcuffing Briggs and bringing him back to Saigon or simply shoving him off a pier wearing concrete boots!"

"I just don't want that slimy excuse for a man to give us the slip again and for us to have to start over looking for him. I have shot stray dogs for much less than what he had done," Klahan said, avoiding the profanity that he wished he felt comfortable using around the colonel. He was able to express himself without restraint when he and John were discussing things alone.

"Son, I'm sure you did the right thing letting him go. Let's just hope he will lead us to a bigger fish than himself before all of this is over. What was so interesting that you wanted to share with me about his partner in crime that he met at the restaurant in Tokyo? Is it someone I would know?"

John and Klahan looked at each other knowingly, and John began.

"Well, sir," John said, "we knew from the wiretap that Michio, the CIA operative in Tokyo, had placed in Briggs' bungalow that Briggs was meeting with someone for lunch, and the discussion between them used so many vague expressions that I just figured it had to be related to the AK-47s that keep showing up back home. So, we thought we would just do a little surveillance on his house and see if we might develop some leads that could help us get to the bottom of all of this theft for arms business. As we were listening to his wiretap, we overhead him say to some unnamed person that he would meet him at the Two Dragons Restaurant in Tokyo the next day for lunch. We wanted to ensure that the least we got accomplished was the identification of his accomplice so we could begin to put everything together."

At this point, John picked up the story. "Klahan and I staked out the restaurant from a distant row of trees, and we observed the people arriving and leaving from the restaurant. We saw this older, distinguished looking gentleman that we both thought we might have seen before go into the restaurant just before Briggs. It was that loud mouth Senator from Maryland who paid you a visit a few months back. Needless to say, we didn't have to do much math to add up what it all probably meant. It appeared to us the SGT Major has some agreement in place with Senator Carlos Carlson."

The colonel was taking all of this new info into his thought process and finally said, "So now we are fishing for the really big fish, gentlemen. This man is extremely dangerous and connected politically at the highest levels of the US Government. I can see now why you wanted to run this by me before we moved in on Briggs. That was a great call by both of you, especially since you probably wanted to kick Briggs' butt for making you work so hard to find him."

John and Klahan just smiled at each other with an acknowledgment of how right and perceptive the colonel had been.

"So where does that leave us, John? Are we going to try and determine who else is involved in this caper before we strike and put them in chains?"

"We spoke to Michio and his pals at the CIA safe house in Saigon, and they suggested that we incorporate a team to watch them until we can determine exactly what they are doing and how they are making it happen. So, as long as they are operating outside of the US mainland, the CIA will take the lead with surveillance and intelligence gathering, and then when they are operating inside the boundaries of the United States, the FBI and NSA will take over. Of course, no one likes to share information from one bureau to another, but we will simply have to cooperate and coordinate our efforts, or these weasels operate right under our noses with no effective data collection or enforcement on our part. That's just unacceptable."

"OK, it sounds like a pretty good and effective plan. Just keep me in the loop anytime there are updates that I need to know about."

"Yes, sir," John said, and he and Klahan left the colonel's office with a sigh of relief.

Chapter 49

Politics and Powerful Weapons

Senator Carlson was able to develop a contact at one of the manufacturing plants where the M-16 assault rifle was constructed. Colt was the first to manufacture the weapon, and before the war in Indo-China was over, millions of the lightweight, but deadly weapons were being manufactured and deployed in Southeast Asia. It had become the standard weapon for the combat soldier, and large quantities of them were floating around like logs on the Mississippi. Carlson knew that with his political and military contacts, he would be able to supply Briggs and his happy band of street fighters with all of the M-16 assault rifles that they would need. He communicated as much back to Briggs with a caveat that "these weapons will cost him $400 each," with Carlson's usual 10% fee on top of the other charges. The senator would work out the details, and the weapons would be delivered and paid for on the same day.

"So, Briggs," the senator said over the long distance telephone line, "we are ready to fill whatever orders for rifles that you have on hand. How many do you need, and when do you need them?"

The SGT Major was startled that this politician could make things happen so quickly. "OK, let me check with my distributor, and I will give you a call later this week with the details on my end," was all Briggs said and then hung up the telephone.

* * * * *

"Jimmy," Briggs said when he was able to connect with his cousin on the telephone, "we need to talk, and I don't mean on the telephone."

"Sure, Cousin, what did you have in mind? I don't really want to fly to Japan just to have a little conversation, if you know what I mean," the young man expressed his opinion in a firm, but calm tone.

"I was thinking that maybe we could meet in the Bahamas and take in a little sun and fun at the same time."

"I like it, Danny," he replied. "What did you have in mind?"

"Let me work out the specifics, and I will send you the details by courier. I would rather not say over the telephone."

"Sure, Cousin, but don't take too long. I have a need for some biscuits really bad. That's why I am assuming you are calling?"

"Just be watching for my express package, and it will tell you all you need to know about our meeting, the time and the place where I will be waiting for you."

"OK, you've got my attention. I will see you soon!"

Briggs had been hearing a slight popping in the telephone line that had concerned him, and he was just about to call the local repairman when he began to wonder if the popping was a bug that had been installed while he was away. Were people listening to his conversations, plotting to take him down?

"I must be fucking paranoid," he thought to himself. He would rather be safe than sorry down the road when he stood a chance to be under arrest for racketeering, grand theft, treason and a few more federal charges that he really didn't want to consider right now. There was a way to check this out, but in the meantime he didn't want to give away his plan to get weapons in the hands of his cousin Jimmy.

Chapter 50

The Slippery Sergeant Major Briggs

Jimmy received a package delivered by the US Post Office a few days after his discussion with his cousin Danny. In it was a bus ticket for a trip to New Orleans and a reservation for the Andrew Jackson Hotel in the French Quarter.

"What the hell?" he thought to himself. "I thought we were meeting in the Bahamas."

*   *   *   *   *

It had been about a week since Jimmy had spoken to his cousin, and he was a little surprised that Danny had changed the plans without calling and giving Jimmy any notice of the change. Since he had not been close to Danny for some time, he wasn't going to read too much into this shift in meeting plans. He would simply have Danny explain why the meeting place had been changed once he was able to sit down with him in Louisiana.

So, Jimmy boarded the bus to New Orleans. He thought that Cousin Danny must be concerned about someone or something to have changed their plans so dramatically from their earlier conversation on their telephone. It was a lengthy ride to The Big Easy for Jimmy when he could just as well have driven down there in his Cadillac or had one of the button men drive him.

"Hell," he thought to himself, "I could have flown down there in a matter of a couple of hours." But, he figured Danny was up to something, so he followed the plan.

*   *   *   *   *

After a very long and tiring bus ride, Jimmy arrived in New Orleans and took a taxi to the Andrew Jackson. He went immediately to the lounge and ordered a double bourbon on the rocks and waited for his cousin to contact him. It took approximately fifteen-minutes for a familiar face to sidle up and sit on a bar stool beside him.

"Jimmy, I'm glad you didn't think that the tickets to New Orleans were a mistake. I am also very pleased that you didn't call me to confirm the change in plans."

"Well, I almost did, but I figured that there must be some serious reason for the change. What's up?"

"When I spoke to you last, I noticed a clicking noise on the telephone line. I was getting ready to call the local telephone company, and then I remembered that when I was at MACV headquarters in Saigon, we occasionally tapped the telephone lines of a suspect. Frequently, there was a popping sound on the line. It wasn't a significant noise, but if you knew what to be listening for, you could pick it up in the background. So, I made a reservation on that telephone for a flight to Nassau and added a hotel room as well. I would bet you there will be federal agents there to arrest us in the Bahamas this evening. Unfortunately for them, we won't be there, and they will be off the trail for a while."

"That's a nice diversion, Cousin Danny. Now what's the current plan for getting some more AK-47s? Did you say our connection was broken in Vietnam? If so, how do we get the rifles here without you being there to run interference?" Danny asked with a puzzled look on his face.

"That's the good news that I didn't want to speak to you about on the telephone. If I am correct and my telephone line is being monitored by the CIA or local Japanese intelligence people, they would find out about our new plan to get automatic weapons into your people's hands. I couldn't take a chance on that happening."

"So now you're here, and you can tell me. It had better be good and quick, or my associates in Dallas will skin me alive, and they'll probably come looking for you as well."

"Don't get in a snit," Briggs told him. "I have it covered. You're going to really like this new plan."

"OK, spill it."

"I have a high ranking contact in the Pentagon who has arranged for us to get American made M-16 assault rifles from a manufacturing plant here in the USA. There will be one less middle-man to pay, and there will be far less chance of our operations being detected by the FBI or NSA."

"Can your guy pull that sort of plan off with reliable results?"

"Oh, yeah. I wish I could tell you who it was, but the less you know about those details, the safer you will be in case you're suspected of cooperating with me."

"I see," he said. "Whatever you think is best, as long as I get the M-16s in a timely manner."

"Consider it done!"

"So when are you returning to Japan, Danny?"

"I'm never going back. That should also throw them off our trail. I just left for the airport with a normal amount of bags, and I will reposition myself here in the States. I have my funds in a safe place that is accessible and untraceable, so I don't have to go back to Kumamoto. They'll look for me and finally figure out that I'm not coming back. That should give me enough time to resettle here."

"Where are you going to relocate? Have you thought about Dallas? That would be convenient for us in our current dealings."

"That's really too convenient, Jimmy. If they trace anything to me or to you, they will have us both. It would be better if you didn't know where I will be. That way, you can't tell them something you really don't know. It's safer for everyone involved in our business deals."

"Like I've thought all along, Danny, you're a genius!"

Chapter 51

A Tricky Trap in Nassau

John and Klahan had been listening to telephone conversations with Briggs and had picked up on an upcoming overseas trip that Briggs had been planning for some time.

John said, "I figure that if we can get as many details as will be available from the telephone calls that we've tapped, we can have someone waiting to pick up Briggs once he has met with his co-conspirators in Nassau. We don't know who Briggs will be meeting, but if we could catch them in the act, we might be able to trace the weapons to the source and their final destination in the US."

"Michio said that his people have overheard Briggs making a reservation for the Sheraton Hotel in Nassau, as well as a flight to the Bahamas on Delta Airlines," Klahan added to John's comments.

"OK, we will have someone at the airport follow Briggs to the hotel, and we can decide at that time if we want to take them into custody or just continue to surveil them. There is a Navy complex on Andros Island that we can operate from, and if necessary, take Briggs and his co-conspirators and hold them for interrogation, assuming we decide that is the best course of action to take."

"It would probably be a good thing to check in with the operations officer there in case we decide to take that course of action. Maybe the colonel can get someone in the Pentagon to set that up for us."

"I think we want to be there, Klahan, to make sure Briggs doesn't give us the slip. I will get the colonel's office to make the necessary travel arrangements for us and send the tickets and hotel reservations to us. I imagine Michio will be happy to let us send that stuff to his office in Tokyo. According to what I've heard so far, the meeting is on tap for later this week."

John and Klahan felt really good about things. They would finally get their man in the Bahamas and take him back to Washington to the Pentagon for interrogation.

Chapter 52

Changing Base of Operations

The first thing that Briggs did when he decided to change his base of operations was to change his identity again.

"Jimmy, do you have a good source for passports, Social Security cards, driver's licenses, and other identification documents? I will want to shed my Joseph Romano identity now that the FBI and other US Government agencies have identified me with it. Can you refer me to someone in Texas who can get that done for me?"

"Sure, Harris County, where Houston is located, is the nation's leading county for fake IDs and Social Security cards. Depending on how much you are willing to pay for the makeover of your documents, they can be good, really good, or almost perfect. Obviously, the more secure they are, the more they cost to execute for the forger. How much are you willing to pay?"

"Let's just say that money is not a problem for me, and I want the best that money can buy. That being the case, who do I contact in Houston to get that done?"

"Well, Cousin, that's not the way it gets done in Texas. You will never meet the forger, and he will never meet you in person. He will work with an intermediary, as you will. That way, it's damn near impossible to trace the person who made your identity papers and how they were delivered to you. There are a few exceptions to that rule, but your situation wouldn't fall into that category. I will mediate for you. Let's just say you'll owe me one for my help."

"OK, so how do I get started?"

"Give me $1000 in cash, and if it costs more than that when it's all finished, we can settle up for the difference. Do you have a preference in a name or nationality?"

"I don't have a name preference, but I do speak fluent Italian, so an Italian heritage would be a natural thing for me. I could speak the language with authority and probably fool a bunch of people if I had to do so. Just don't give me the name Danny or Jimmy," he laughed.

"What do you think about 'Alberto Deodatus Rizzo' for your name?"

"It sounds fine to me, what does it mean?"

"Well, Alberto means bright nobility, Deodatus was a name given to many saints, and Rizzo means curly hair. In other words, you are 'a bright and noble saint with curly hair!'" Jimmy laughed, and that even brought a chuckle to Briggs. "Hey, it's a good name, and no one would ever be able to trace you from the name alone."

"OK, so I will be a curly-haired saint if that will help me hide from the authorities. Let's get the documents ordered. How long do you think it will take to get them done? I need to move on to my new place as soon as possible. I feel exposed here in New Orleans with my current ID and papers."

"I'm just guessing, but I imagine we will have you on the road in a couple of days. Is that fast enough for you?"

"That's fine. I will be staying at the Andrew Jackson Hotel in the French Quarter until the documents are ready."

"OK. I'll get this handled and get back to you as soon as everything is complete. By the way, can you return the favor by finding out when the first batch of M-16 assault rifles will be ready for transfer to us?"

"Sure, I can probably find that out for you in a couple of days. We can exchange the information when my documents are ready."

"Just call me on my office number at 703-555-1243 and tell whoever answers the phone that my cousin needs to speak to me about an important matter, and I will take it from there. I will call the hotel, and we can determine how to pass the information to each other at that time."

"That sounds doable. Remember, money is not a problem for me, but lingering too long and having the CIA or NSA find me while I am waiting for the identity documents would hurt us both."

"I will make it a priority."

PART IV: CLOSING IN ON THE PREY

Chapter 53

There's No Place Like Home

It took about forty-eight hours to complete, but Danny Briggs was now Alberto Deodatus Rizzo.

"Danny," Cousin Jimmy said, "you are now Alberto. You need to think of yourself as Alberto. The only way to make this work successfully is for you to assimilate yourself into this new identity. You grew up in Los Angeles and later moved to San Diego when your father was assigned to the North Island Naval Air Station. The family had originally immigrated to the Unites States at the turn of the twentieth century from Tuscany, Italy, during the great migration of Europeans after World War I."

"Your father served in the US Navy during WW II and returned home to San Diego, California, to build his business and raise his family. There were three children in the Rizzo family, and you were the eldest. You joined the US Navy in 1958 when you graduated from San Diego State University and became a Lieutenant JG and served all of your military time in the US territories. You never served an overseas assignment, and you later returned to San Diego, where you currently reside. Do you have any questions?"

"How did you get all of that done in a span of a couple of days?" Briggs asked. "I am assuming there are credentials for all of that stuff in the file you are holding?"

"Every document you need to identify with Alberto is in this file. Your new California driver's license, a new US Passport, a Social Security card with a legitimate account number, and other minor documents that you will find helpful are included."

"So how much more do I owe you, Cousin?"

"Let's just say that you owe me a favor or two in the future. I may never call those favors in, but if I do, I will expect your unwavering cooperation. Are we in agreement?"

"Sure," Briggs said and took the folder from Cousin Jimmy. "I guess I need to return home to San Diego," Briggs said with a smile.

Twenty-four hours after that conversation, Briggs was checking into a hotel under his old identity, Joseph Romano. He didn't want his new credentials spoiled with traceable facts, and he would ditch the Romano identity soon enough. Even if someone came looking for Joseph Romano, the trail would go cold quickly in a city that numbered seven hundred thousand in a county that had a population exceeding one million people.

"I need to buy a house for cash so there will be no paper trail," he thought to himself. "Then, I will need to open simple bank account, a couple of store credit card accounts, get a residential telephone line, and all of the routine things a homeowner normally does. I will be so normal that even I wouldn't recognize me!" He chuckled to himself at his approach to this new identity.

Now, Briggs needed to contact the senior senator from Maryland about some M-16 assault rifles.

Chapter 54

Missing in Action

"Embarrassing," John swore to Klahan, "you might use a little more hostile language than that!" He was referring to the fact that Briggs did not deplane in Nassau, nor did he or anyone associated with him check into the hotel.

"How did he figure out that we were onto him?" Klahan asked. "I mean, we were real careful in our surveillance in Japan, and we never even approached him or the senator. I can't figure this one out."

"Somehow, some way, Briggs got wind of Michio and his people tracking him before he left Kumamoto. I don't know how yet, but that has to be what happened. And, if I were a betting man, I would bet you that Japan has seen the last of SGT Major Briggs!" John said with disgust.

"So how do we get another lead on him? How could he just disappear from the face of the Earth?"

"It makes me wonder if he's getting some outside help from someone. This has gone too smoothly all along for Briggs to be doing all of this from Japan or Saigon or wherever he's been in the past. He has to have someone in the US helping him. Let's get the FBI and NSA to track every distant relative of Briggs and see if we can figure out how he's staying one step ahead of us."

Klahan called the colonel's office to report on the way Briggs gave everyone the slip in Nassau. He was ready to be blasted by Forsett, but instead he just heard a little laugh from the old man.

"Now that's one sneaky little bastard. I will give him credit for his craftiness, but we have to find him and stop his treachery. It appears to my field commanders that the security leak is no longer a problem and that whatever Briggs was doing over here may be over. That doesn't hold true for the homeland. He's still up to something criminal. I am sure that he has simply shifted his emphasis from getting weapons from Vietnam to getting them somewhere in the US. I am going to cut orders for you and John to be attached to the US Marine Base in Quantico, Virginia, until we get this matter resolved. Please check in with me and give me updates when you think I need to know what's happening over there. Briggs may have escaped my command and the Southeast Asia area, but he won't escape you and John. Tell me I am correct about that, Klahan."

"Yes, sir. We will find Briggs and bring him to justice!"

"Atta-boy, Klahan. I knew I could count on you two to finish the job. And, by the way, if Briggs disappears during all of this craziness, I won't care one bit. As far as I am concerned, you and John can be the judge, jury and executioner of that fat little bastard!"

"Yes, sir, Colonel, we will handle it and get back with you with the details."

"Good, Klahan. You two should watch your backs. That little son-of-a-bitch is sneaky as hell, and I wouldn't trust him as far as I could throw him."

"Klahan," John said after he had hung up the telephone from his call with the colonel, "let's get on a flight to FBI headquarters in Washington. I will get the colonel to put in a call to one of his many friends there to give us an introduction. I don't think we can trace Briggs without some help from the FBI and the NSA. You know the CIA is prohibited from operating out in the open inside the continental United States, so our connections there will be of little help once we have touched down in Washington." With that, John rang the colonel back and explained what they intended to do next and received the colonel's blessing.

John and Klahan went back to the Nassau airport and caught a direct flight to Washington. They arrived in the middle of the afternoon, and by dinner time they had been introduced to a number of agents with the FBI. They had decided that they would trace Briggs through the FBI, no matter how long it was going to take.

Chapter 55

Southern California is the Place to Live

After living in a rain-soaked country for a couple of years, living in Southern California was a dream! Rain was somewhat of an inconvenience at times, but it was not a way of life to the San Diego residents, as it was in Southeast Asia. Briggs could get accustomed to this new lifestyle pretty quickly.

"How soon can I move into the condo?" Briggs questioned the real estate agent as he looked over the paperwork that he had just signed on the condo overlooking the marina on Anchorage Lane.

"Well," she said with a happy smile, "since this is a cash transaction, you can move in as soon as the closing attorney executes the paperwork with the county clerk. I would say in about a couple of weeks."

"OK, please let me know as soon as it is official, and I will begin moving into my place. I am excited to be living so near the water and in such a lovely area of San Diego."

"We are sure you will like it here, Mr. Rizzo," she reassured him in her best professional, real estate voice. "Where did you say you lived prior to buying the condo?"

"New Orleans."

"Well, please feel free to contact me at any time if you have further questions about the property or the city." With that comment, she had packed up the contracts and headed for her car. Within minutes, he was back at his hotel room, trying to decide how to keep a low profile until his new home was ready. It didn't mean that he could wait two weeks to get the new shipment of rifles underway. He would deal with that issue in the morning.

"Hey, Cousin Danny," Briggs heard Jimmy say when he answered the telephone in Dallas the next morning. "I hope you are calling to talk about those biscuits we have been discussing." Jimmy had told Briggs that the code word for guns or rifles was biscuits, and he hoped that John had remembered that detail. You just never knew who might be listening in on one of your conversations these days.

"Yes, Jimmy, that's why I am calling. I will be checking with my supplier today, and I should be able to give you a pretty good idea when the biscuits can be delivered in the next day or so."

"How many biscuits do you think you can get for us?"

"Hopefully, I can get one thousand to start. I will let you know for sure in a day or two. They will cost about twice as much as the last biscuits. Is that going to be a problem for you?"

"The price is fine. What we need to do is expedite them as much as possible. Can you get that done for me?"

"Absolutely," Briggs answered without equivocation. "Consider it done!"

"That's what I like to hear. Call me when they are on the way to us."

Briggs hung up the telephone and felt like he had just gotten refocused on his top priority—getting the rifles to his cousin for a nice profit to himself. He could get accustomed to this arrangement.

The next call that Briggs needed to make was to his contact for the M-16 assault rifles. The senator would not like being leaned on by him, but unless Briggs was mistaken, he had that blowhard over a barrel.

Briggs dialed the senator's office. "Senator Carlson's office, how can I help you today?" the congenial voice on the other end of the telephone line answered.

"I would like to speak to the senator, please," Briggs spoke into the receiver when the administrative assistant had completed her usual speech about the senator not being available.

186

"Sir, I'm not sure that the senator is even in his office, much less available to speak to you on the telephone."

"Just tell him his favorite sergeant is on the line for him."

"Oh, I remember you from an earlier call. I will get him for you, sir, without delay." Within a minute or two, Briggs heard the senator pick up the line.

"Thanks, Nancy," the senator said to his assistant. "I will take it from here. Please make doubly sure that we are not disturbed."

"Yes, sir," Nancy said and hung up her extension of the telephone.

Now, the conversation could go on as usual. The senator's telephone line was a secure line, and no one would be listening in on his telephone calls in the Pentagon.

"Senator," Briggs got straight to the point, "we are going to need one thousand of those M-16 rifles delivered ASAP. How soon can you get them shipped to my contact in Dallas, Texas?"

"My guy can get them on the truck in twenty-four hours, but the payment will need to be wired into his bank before he will let the truck leave for your destination. Is that going to be a problem?"

"Nope," he said, "not a problem at all."

"OK, Briggs, what do you need from me to get the money transferred?"

"We just need a bank routing number and any pertinent information that the bank will require to accept the funds that we will transfer."

"It's on the way to you in a Western Union wire. You should have it within the hour."

"I expect the volume to pick up considerably over the next few weeks and months. You need to line me up five thousand rifles a month to ship to the same destination until further notice. I will wire the money into your bank account two days before you have to ship the weapons so you can verify that the funds are there."

"That sounds reasonable, Briggs, even for you."

Chapter 56

The Secret to Shipping M-16 Assault Rifles

The M-16 assault rifles that were manufactured and shipped to overseas battle areas were made in Connecticut. Senator Carlos Carlson had been a great friend of Lance Berryman, the current senator from Connecticut, and that senator owed Carlson some big-time favors. It was time to call in some of those favors, so Carlson picked up the telephone and dialed his friend.

"Lance," Carlson spoke into the telephone, "Carlson here. I need to set up a meeting with you outside of the Beltway. Maybe we can meet at a small restaurant in Falls Church, Virginia, sometime tomorrow. It's urgent that we speak."

"Well, Carlos, I already have plans for lunch tomorrow. Maybe we can get together later this week?"

"Lance," Carlson put some steel into the tone of his voice, "we need to meet now. It's in both of our interests to meet immediately. Unless you have figured out a way to get the Russians to tear down the Berlin Wall, you need to meet me tomorrow—got it?"

"OK, I will be there. There is a nice, quiet Italian restaurant off the square across from the county courthouse. Let's meet there at 1:00 PM for lunch. How does that sound to you?"

"Fine, Lance, I will be there."

*   *   *   *   *

Briggs showed up at 12:30 PM at the courthouse square and found the restaurant that Lance had suggested. He went inside, found a secluded booth in the rear of the restaurant, sat down and ordered a bourbon and water on the rocks. It was early to be drinking, but he was going to need it before his day was over.

"I will sit with my friend back in the corner," Lance told the waiter when he entered the restaurant and saw Briggs sitting in a booth in the back. "You can bring me a glass of Bordeaux and a menu."

"Yes, sir." The waiter bowed graciously to the senators and went off in search of an expensive bottle of wine for their table. He actually enjoyed these big-time senators and congressmen coming into his small bar acting bigger than life. He always found a way to profit from their lack of humility.

"So what is so important that we needed to meet today and not one day next week?" asked Lance.

"I need a favor—a very big favor from you, and there cannot be any questions from you why it has to be done this way."

Looking at Carlson suspiciously, Lance asked, "What kind of favor, Carlos?" almost afraid of the answer he might get in return.

"The Colt Manufacturing Plant in your state makes M-16 assault rifles for the Department of Defense and ships them all over the world. I need to add another destination for rifles to the plant's existing list, and your office can make that happen for me. The payment for the rifles will be made by the terminal receiving them. You can designate the location as an anti-espionage unit, or you can label them a counter-intelligence unit operating undercover. I don't really care how you do it, but you need to get it done today or tomorrow and get one thousand rifles shipped to an address I will give you today."

"Are you out of your mind, Carlson? It is a serious offense if we get caught selling automatic rifles to anyone other than the US military. I don't know if I can pull that off, much less in a day or two."

"You owe me big-time, Berryman, for saving your ass with your wife and family. I would hate to think that my recollection of your alibi for the night that young page was raped and murdered would have to be altered because I forgot that you really weren't with me at the Playboy Club in Baltimore that evening."

"OK, OK," Lance almost screamed. "I will get it done. But really, Carlos, I didn't have anything to do with that girl's rape and murder. You have to believe me!"

"Personally, Lance, I don't give a shit if you did or didn't have anything to do with that poor girl. What I know is that you were banging her in your senatorial office twice a week, and the rumor was that she was pregnant and looking for an abortion or some way to get rid of the baby. That's all I know, and really, all I need to know. Just make this deal happen, and your story stays safe with me."

"Right," Lance answered with a bit of frustration showing on his face. "I'll have it set up tomorrow. I will get your rifles shipped within the week."

"Good man, Lance," Carlos said with satisfaction. "I knew I could count on you!" Carlson got up, shook Lance's hand, and was out the door, heading for his office on Capitol Hill.

Chapter 57

How to Trace the Untraceable

"We're sitting in plush chairs around a mahogany conference table in the heart of the FBI building. That much is a fact—that much we know. Beyond that, I'm not sure we know even what we think we know about Briggs. There's something missing in his background check that I'm sure if we could determine exactly what it is, we could get some more credible leads on him." John was thinking out loud, and his thoughts were pretty much the same ones that Klahan had, but he had just not expressed them.

"John, let's take an inventory of what we know and what we don't know about Briggs."

It was very obvious to both John and Klahan that Briggs was smart and had a calculating mind that would match any super spy agent the CIA or FBI had ever trained.

"Briggs is not flying by the seat of his pants on this deal," John said to Klahan. "As much as I dislike what the man is doing to expose our country to dangerous weapons, as well as his negligence for the potential loss of life because of his weapons for information scheme, you have to admire his ability to stay one or two steps ahead of us."

"We can admire his skill at being a thief and traitor, but we need to catch him to stop the terrible fallout that will come when all of those weapons hit the American streets. I didn't grow up here, nor do I know a lot about the culture, but from what I read in the newspapers and magazines, the only market for automatic rifles in the USA is with the mobs or gangs. Am I correct?"

"You are correct, my friend. We do need to catch Briggs, and we will. It just amazes me that he is so good at being really bad," John said.

Klahan just nodded his head in an affirmative way to let John know that as much as he disliked Briggs, he had to agree with his incredible timing and ability to evade hundreds of people looking for him twenty-four hours a day.

"So how do we begin tracing this guy, John?"

"We've been looking at this all wrong, Klahan," John said with a thoughtful expression on his face. "What we are missing here is that we don't know who else is making it feasible for Briggs to keep making these moves that keep him a step ahead of us. We need to start investigating Briggs as if we had no knowledge about his past in Vietnam or Japan. How would we go about that if we were starting from scratch today? That's the question we need to answer to make real progress and get ahead of that little bugger!"

Klahan opened the FBI and NSA files on Briggs and used the overhead projector to project the images of the documents on the wall screen so they could see the forms better and both examine them at the same time.

"What we know," John looked at the background research that the FBI had collected on Briggs, "is that he grew up in the Dallas area, got into some trouble from time to time and essentially had to join the military to keep from going to jail or JUVY. He had a good, solid Catholic upbringing until he was kicked out of a Catholic parochial school for attempting to kill a fellow student. The question we need to ask is, 'What or who is not represented here that had an influence on him in the past, or even currently?' That's really the question."

"Briggs appears to have been an only child. So, if there were no other kids in the family and he didn't seem to get along very well with the other kids at school, just who did he confide in, and could they still be an influence on his actions now that he is an adult?"

"Good thinking, Klahan. Let's comb over all of the documents and see if there is anything that might produce a lead for us in his early childhood." With that, they divided up the documents and reports that had been compiled on Briggs and began to try to relate anyone or anything from his past to his present situation. There simply had to be a connection somewhere.

"Hey, John, look at this. Briggs had a cousin in Dallas that he hung out with once he was kicked out of the Catholic high school. From these reports, it appears this cousin Jimmy Garrison was in and out of JUVY a good bit of time while Briggs was hanging out with him. Do you think that his cousin may be the one he has reconnected with now that he really needs a friend?"

"That's a good pick up, Klahan. Let's check out this cousin Jimmy Garrison and see how he has turned out. It's been twenty years since they were kids playing together in the 'hood."

"Just for kicks, let's run Jimmy Garrison's name through the files and see if we get a hit on anything recent that indicates that Jimmy has been less than a model citizen."

Just recently, the FBI and the NSA had received new computer technology that could sort through information a thousand times faster than humans, and John and Klahan were anxious to put the new technology to work for them on the Briggs' case.

"To tell you the truth," John had expressed his truthful feelings to the operator of the IBM 360 mainframe computer that was taking up a mid-sized room in the FBI Headquarters building, "I have no idea of how this new technical approach to research works. However, I am willing to give it a good test if it can help us narrow down how we might catch SGT Major Briggs."

The technician seemed to have his head somewhere else because he didn't even acknowledge John's comments. He simply set out with data punch cards that represented every possible amount of information in regards to Briggs, fed them into the huge computer, and picked up the card in a sorted order once the machine had done its work. There was also a printout that organized all of the data into a written summary that became a timeline for the events in Briggs' life from the earliest information known on him in the files through the data that was indicated on his latest bogus trip to the Bahamas.

"I'm super impressed," John said after reading the report that the technician gave both him and Klahan. "This is almost scary," he continued. "I can see the future being a place where 'you can run, but you cannot hide' if this machine is the beginning of intelligence gathering and compilation on individuals."

Klahan and John took a coffee break and sat down with the report in the breakroom of the FBI building. As they both read the report, they both came to the same conclusion within minutes of each other.

"It appears that we may need to take a trip to Dallas, Texas, soon. What do you think, Klahan?"

"I absolutely agree with your assessment, John. However, there is something that is troubling to me about this potential Dallas connection of Briggs."

"What's that, Klahan?" John asked when they both had finished reading and rereading the report on Briggs and his Dallas history.

"Again, I can only refer to what I have read in books and magazines about the culture of these large American cities. However, it appears that Briggs' best friend and distant cousin is connected with the organized crime family that is headquartered in Dallas. I think we need to run a complete background investigation on this Jimmy Garrison, as well as anyone else who may have been an influence on Briggs during his early years in Dallas."

"That's another great idea, Klahan. Damn if you're not becoming a super sleuth spy right before my eyes! Seriously, Klahan, you are really a natural at this type of research. Remind me not to get on your bad side, or I could never live down the dirt you might find in my past!" John laughed.

"I think our next move is to consult with the FBI and NSA directors to see if we need to be working with them in regards to this Jimmy Garrison in Dallas. They may currently have some surveillance going on in Dallas, and we don't need to muck up a lot of work that they have already done on this crime family."

"I agree. Let's make an appointment with the FBI director and see where it takes us."

They both closed their folders and decided that the most important thing to do at this point was to find a respectable restaurant for dinner—and a not so respectable bar for their nightcap.

Chapter 58

The Dallas Crime Family Hierarchy

The Dallas crime syndicate had its early roots in Italy, where most of the Mafia or Costa Nostra originated, and very few people in the Dallas-Ft. Worth area had any clue that the organization had such an impact on things that were happening in the Metropolitan Dallas area. A very good reason for that was that those organizations were targeting other crime families and certain businesses that were prone to be involved in shady dealings and that operated just outside of the law.

"You can live in Dallas, Texas, all of your life and never come in contact with anyone involved in the crime families of the Mafia or Costa Nostra," one of the federal prosecutors had said in a public statement in the early 1960s. "However, if you are involved in criminal activity, you will be very involved in many aspects of these family operations. That's just the way that kind of business is transacted in Dallas, Texas, and most other major crime syndicate cities."

It wasn't a secret to the local police or the state police, but the federal boys went a step further and did their best to root out the "bad elements" in the business community. They usually failed miserably.

The Savoca Family had been trying to get the upper hand on their competition for years—the street gangs and the other crime families in neighboring states. They saw the potential of elevating the Savoca Family's influence in the entire southwest by brokering a deal that would create an imbalance in power when automatic weapons were concerned. This move, if successful, would give Jimmy the chance to put himself in line for the top management of the Savoca Family when Salvatore was no longer able to command the family's affairs. After just a few weeks of negotiating with his Cousin Danny, he was poised to make that happen.

*   *   *   *   *

"Jimmy, we are ready to ship you one thousand biscuits immediately. What I need you to do is to wire the money for these biscuits into a new bank using the routing number that I will give you today. When we are together again, I will explain why that has to happen before I can get these biscuits headed your way."

"OK, Cousin Danny. Give me the info, and I will handle it. What is the cost per unit of these biscuits?"

"The last time you paid $2 per biscuit; this time it will be $4 each. These biscuits are much higher in quality. I'm sure you will be happy with the results."

$4 per biscuit meant $400 per M-16 rifle. It was a simple code that the crime family used, and although the FBI knew what the code implied, they could not arrest anyone for planning to sell biscuits for $4 each. Instead of trying to hide the transactions from the electronic snooping devices, the mafia simply would not implicate themselves in any way that they were negotiating for anything other than food.

"OK, then," Jimmy responded in a few minutes. "I will wire $4,000 into your account today. Please give me the routing number, and I will handle it."

Briggs gave a number to Jimmy over the telephone line, and the FBI thought that they had just received a break and could trace the money that way. When Briggs and Jimmy had last spoken together in New Orleans, however, they had devised a way to code numbers so the FBI would have a hard time unscrambling them. It seemed to be working well so far.

"Thanks, Jimmy, and consider the transaction completed as of today," Briggs said.

John and Klahan were made aware that the FBI had Jimmy Garrison of Dallas, Texas, under surveillance and about the conversation that they had overheard on the tapped call. John and Klahan were going to be on the next flight to Dallas. This might be a break that could lead to Briggs' eventual capture.

Chapter 59

A Move from Saigon to Dallas

Tuyen was very lonely now that Klahan was in the United States, and it appeared to her that he might never come home. She missed him terribly and had written to him on numerous occasions that she wanted him to come home to Saigon.

"Tuyen," he spoke into the telephone after he had read her last letter, "I am involved with John Bremen in a manhunt for SGT Major Briggs, and I just can't leave now."

"Then see if the colonel or one of your many new American friends can send me to America to be with you," she pleaded.

"That may not be as easy as you make it out to sound, little Angel. This is a mission and not a pleasure trip for me and John. I will run it by John and see if he thinks we can make it happen, but please don't get too excited until we find out if it is even possible."

"Please let me know soon. I am willing to close up the Steam and Cream and move out of this war-torn country!" she cried.

"OK, Tuyen. I will see what we can get done. I will call you as soon as I have information for you."

*   *   *   *   *

John and Klahan had flown to Dallas to establish a monitoring site for the purposes of tracking down Briggs. Klahan was waiting for the exact moment when he thought he could mention Tuyen's request to come to America for a visit.

"So, Klahan," John addressed him at breakfast, "did you speak to Tuyen on the telephone last night? I know that she has been trying to reach you for the last few days. What did she have to say?"

"She is very lonely, John. She wants to come to America to visit while I am away from Saigon. She hoped you might be able to get the colonel in Saigon or one of our new American friends in the FBI or NSA to arrange a temporary visit for her while I am deployed here. I know that is asking a lot, especially since she is not a citizen of this country, but she helped the United States fight espionage to try and track down Briggs."

"Klahan, I don't see any reason why that would be too difficult a challenge to get done. We need to establish a base of operations in Dallas anyway. We can simply rent an apartment with an extra bedroom. The State Department can issue a temporary travel visa for her, and she can stay with you until we return to Saigon and give our report to Colonel Forsett. I will call the colonel and also ask the FBI to help us on this end. As soon as I am assured that they will make it happen, you can tell Tuyen. Let's not tell her anything at this point, so she won't be upset if they don't approve it. I don't think there will be a problem."

"That's great, John. I'm sure Tuyen will be in your debt forever if you pull this off for her."

"I will do what I can. In the meantime, let's begin looking for an apartment or house for rent in the East Dallas area. From what I understand from the FBI, East Dallas is where the local Mafia has its operations and where we will be most effective in our search for Briggs."

*   *   *   *   *

They spent two days with a local real estate agent looking at apartments, houses, and even condominiums for rent before they found the ideal unit. It had four bedrooms, a large kitchen, two bathrooms, and a nice living room/dining room combination. That would allow each of them to have a separate bedroom, a separate bath for Tuyen from the guys, and a place for Tuyen to stay busy cooking Vietnamese dinners for them in the evening. Now all they needed was the final approval from the State

Department, and Tuyen could apply for her visa and head to Dallas. The final approval came the next day from the colonel's office with a note attached to the visa application that simply read, "You both owe me, boys!" They got a laugh from the colonel's humorous note. He was not usually that informal with any of his men.

"Tuyen," she heard Klahan's voice say, "you are coming to Dallas, Texas, to stay with me while I am in this country. Start packing your things because you will be leaving in two days to join me."

"I am very happy, Klahan. Thank you so much, and thank John as well for letting me come to America."

Now it was time to turn their undivided focus on the Dallas crime family and Jimmy Garrison.

Chapter 60

Tuning in on the Crime Syndicate

A week had passed since John, Klahan, and Tuyen had gotten settled into the large apartment on the east side of Dallas. Tuyen had been granted a temporary visa, and she had been allowed to apply for a permanent visa because of the possibility of personal danger should she return to Saigon.

"I think she has a good case for the Immigration and Naturalization Service to consider. There is obviously a link to her and her family since they were methodically hunted down and murdered when the Battle of Hua was initiated by the Viet Cong and the NVA. We will know within a few months how her application is being handled, and it is possible that the colonel or someone else in the Pentagon can help as well."

This made Tuyen feel much better, and her personality began to return to its normal, easy-going nature after just a few days in Dallas.

"So, Tuyen, are you looking to find a big, brave American to sweep you off of your feet and marry you? You know if that happens, you get to stay in the US forever!" Klahan said to her with a twinkle in his eye.

"Oh, no," Tuyen said, blushing from head to toe. I am not looking for a husband. I just want to live in a place where I can go to sleep with the assurance that I will wake up the next morning not thinking that I might be a target for the NVA that day."

"You are safe here," Klahan reassured her. "We will keep you protected, and you will not have to go back to Vietnam unless you want to do so," he told her.

*   *   *   *   *

John and Klahan were busy setting up surveillance equipment for the sting that they had planned. They had been given information that the Italian establishment known as Alfredo's Market and Restaurant on South Beltline Road was a front for the Savoca Family. It was a pretty good bet that money laundering was going on there, as well as in several of the self-service laundry outlets in the southeast portion of Dallas County. The Savoca family owned a number of laundry outlets, as well as hand-rubbed car detail shops in the Dallas area. All of these businesses were suspected of laundering drug money for the crime family, and there was so much cash money that was collected and deposited in the local banks that this was a natural front for such activities. It would be hard to prove, however, without wire taps and other electronic surveillance, but Klahan and John would definitely keep an eye on these places for Jimmy "The Hammer" Garrison and his wayward cousin Danny Briggs.

*   *   *   *   *

"I just need a court order to listen in on their telephone calls and to bug the restaurant for information that will corroborate our current intelligence on this crime family," John was telling the District Attorney's office. "We have a lot of circumstantial evidence that we can prove as fact once we can get the family to admit to on hidden tape. That's all we need, sir."

"Oh, really, Mr. Bremen? All you need is to spy on someone without a justifiable reason? And, I assume, that makes sense to you, sir?"

"Look," John continued, "these are bad people. They kill people, and they smuggle in drugs and weapons that kill even more people when they are used to commit crimes!" John was beginning to raise his voice a little in his response to the prosecutor.

"Look, Mr. Bremen, there are many bad people in this world. However, if those supposedly bad people live in the United States of America, in Dallas County, they have constitutional rights. You are asking me to ignore the US Constitution because you think there are some bad people who you want to surveil? Your search warrant and surveillance equipment requests are denied. If you want me or any sitting judge in the State of Texas, to give you carte blanche opportunities over the rights of another individual, you best bring us more than an opinion. You are wasting my time. Please leave my office, and take your petitions with you!" the ADA almost screamed.

"Well, that didn't go so well," Klahan said to John once they were in the elevator descending to the lobby of the District Attorney's office building. "I think we just got told!"

"It's just a little setback, Klahan. We cannot let these local people drag their feet and keep us from completing our job—a job that I don't need to remind you is paramount in preventing an all out street war here in America."

Klahan looked at John a little skeptically. "So how do we get the authority to act without the District Attorney to allow us to listen in on their conversations? If we wire-tap them and find something that they are doing illegal, then we can't use that information because it would not be allowable in court, could we?"

John just smiled and said to Klahan, "Oh, ye of little faith, Klahan. There's more than one way to skin a cat!"

"I simply do not understand that statement. What does skinning a cat have to do with our need to tap into their telephone line? You Americans have so many sayings that just don't make sense to me at all!" Klahan shook his head and looked at John with frustration.

"I keep forgetting that you come from a culture where when you make a statement, it is usually a statement of fact. We in America use expressions like that to make a point. When I say, 'It's raining cats and dogs,' it means that it is raining so hard that it appears that the animals are falling out of the sky. Do you understand what I'm saying?" He looked at Klahan.

"No, John. How can it rain cats and dogs? They are too heavy to be picked up in the humidity and then rained down on another area. It just makes no sense at all to me."

John couldn't help but laugh a little at his friend and colleague. "I promise not to use idioms like that in the future. Besides, it takes too long to explain the intended meaning to you!" He slapped Klahan on the back and assumed he would understand the gesture.

"This is one crazy country, John," Klahan said and just shook his head. "But seriously, John, how can we get the authority to perform the surveillance and tape their conversations?"

"This is a great opportunity for me to explain how our form of government works in this country. For every level of legal authority, there is another level higher where you can appeal your case if you feel that there is merit in your request. For instance, we appealed to the Dallas County District Attorney's Office for a wiretap authorization. Since they denied us the authority to proceed with what we need to do, we now appeal the decision by the county District Attorney to the State of Texas court system. If they uphold the county's decision, then we appeal to the State Supreme Court, and so on up the ladder."

"But wouldn't it be pretty useless if this dragged on long enough for the criminals to find out about the surveillance? They could simply feed us some nonsense, and we would be none the wiser."

"That would be an affirmative, Klahan. So we do the next best thing."

"What is that?"

"We call in the FBI and get them to do the dirty work for us with the promise that they get credit for the final take-down, if and when that happens. We get our info, it is sanctioned by the US Government and the FBI, and we stop the traitor and get him locked up for the rest of his miserable life."

"Will that work?"

"It's definitely worth a try, wouldn't you agree?"

"Yes, I would agree."

John picked up the telephone and called the FBI director's office in Washington. It took a few minutes for him to wade through the gate-keepers that were there to screen the many calls a day that came into the FBI switchboard. He knew that eventually he might get to tell his story, and for that opportunity he would wait as long as it took.

Chapter 61

It's Time to Move Some Weapons

The weather was about as nice as anyone could ever want in San Diego. This was like living in Paradise. The temperature was never higher than 80 degrees, and it never was any lower than 55 degrees, even in the dead of winter. Besides the almost perfect climate, the women were beautiful, and Briggs had not seen a shy one since he landed here. He had to pinch himself every now and then to make sure he had not died and gone to Heaven.

"Hey, Jimmy?" Briggs said to his cousin over the telephone line. "Did you get the shipment of the biscuits OK last week?"

"Yes, we got them. They were the best biscuits you have sent so far. Can we expect to continue to have that type of biscuits from now on?"

"Absolutely, you can expect the best from me. If my supply of these special biscuits is impacted in any way, I will find another source for you. Right now, I don't see a problem at all on the horizon."

"Well, that's good to know. Can you increase the amount you ship this time by 100%? We really need them as soon as possible."

"I'll get right on it. As soon as your money is wired into my account, we will get them ready for shipment."

"That's great. I think this is going to be a very good partnership."

"We aim to please," Briggs said ironically. He didn't even figure that he had made a Freudian slip until after he had hung up the telephone.

He called Senator Carlson and was put through to him quickly for the first time that he had been dealing with him on the M-16 rifles.

"So, Carlos, how are things back in Washington?"

"They are fine, and I have no complaints. Why are you calling me, Briggs? Is there some problem that I am not aware of that we need to address?"

"No, there's nothing like that, Carlos. We have a very happy customer who wants to increase his allotment of rifles by 100% and is willing to pay for them."

"Look, Briggs," the senator said with a little irritation, "I don't have the authority to increase the shipment of these firearms. All of that has to go through the senator from Connecticut's office, and he is not as good a friend to me as you might imagine. It may be difficult to do."

"You will just have to lean on him, Carlos. If you lean on him, I will not have to lean on you. You know how this works. You choose the lesser evil to avoid the larger evil. In your case, I am the larger evil!" he said as he raised his voice. I don't need to leak any information to the Joint Chief's office about our little deal in Saigon, do I?"

"Let me talk to him and see if he will work with me on this Briggs. I'm telling you, this guy is a stickler for details, and I already have him out on a pretty long limb."

"Just get it done, Carlson. You really have no choice!"

* * * * *

Senator Carlson called the office of Senator Berryman. "Lance, we need to talk. I need for you to up the number of rifles to the company down in Dallas by 100%, and I need it done now."

"Hey, Carlson, I can't get that done without raising a lot of eyebrows in the Congress. You just don't understand 'no' when you hear it, do you?"

"I understand that you will go to jail if you make me tell the truth about the night that poor page girl went missing while you were unaccountable. Do you really want that to come out, Lance?"

"You're going to push me too far one of these days, Carlos, and it won't go down good for you."

"Is that a threat, Lance?"

"I'm just telling you that you are skating on thin ice with these constant threats. It could get you in trouble."

"Just get it done, Lance. I don't care how or who you have to screw over to get it done, but get it done now!" he demanded.

*   *   *   *   *

The senator from Connecticut had not risen to the top of the political ladder by being timid. He had friends, who had friends, and so on. One of those friends was a shady character who worked for one of Berryman's political supporters.

"I have this guy who is driving me nuts with all of the arm twisting and threatening comments that goes along with high-handed dealings. He keeps threatening to expose my indiscrete affair some years back if I don't continue to support him. I need this situation handled. Can you get someone to do it?"

"Oh, yes, Senator. All I need in return is the Highway Bill passed so our area can get some of those federal dollars. Can I assume you will hold up your end of the bargain if I handle your problem?"

"You can consider that bill will be pushed through the Senate with no unusual delays."

"Then we have a deal!"

Chapter 62

Jimmy Garrison's Place in the Family

It was obvious to anyone paying attention that Jimmy Garrison was moving up in the Savoca crime family in Dallas. His uncle had been the Don, and Jimmy had learned the ropes of the business by working with him after school and in the summers without his mom and dad knowing about it. He was a runner for the crime family until he was about fourteen years old, and then Uncle John gave him a block of the neighborhood to manage. He would hustle the owners of the businesses and, when necessary, would call in some of the family's muscle if the owners of the businesses would not pay up on time.

"Hey, kid," Uncle John would call to him, "are you going to come into the business with me or listen to the priest and your folks and become a goodie-two-shoes and go to church and college and all of that crap?"

"No, Uncle John, I want to work for you. My folks just won't let me, and they keep watching me like a hawk."

"Well, we need to fix that kid, don't we? I'll tell you what you need to do. You get some kid at your school to pick a fight with you in front of a lot of witnesses, and then you beat him until they think you're going to kill him. The Catholic Church will throw you out of school, and we can begin our serious training at that time."

And the rest is history, as they say. The transfer to the public schools failed miserably, and Jimmy was out on the streets learning the business from the ground up. It took him a few months before he ran into Joey the Knife, and Joey brought him into the fold, just like Uncle John had told him to do.

"I tried to join the US Army, but they said I had flat feet, and they wouldn't take me. I wanted to get my hands on one of those M-16 assault rifles and kill me some Viet Cong," he said.

"Screw them!" Jimmy said belligerently. "I don't need the Army to make my mark."

"You do as I say, kid, and I'll get you to captain before you know it," Joey had told Jimmy when he recruited him. "You have to learn the business by being on the street, and you have to earn some credibility with your family members. No one respects you if you are weak and incompetent."

Jimmy had done those things, and now he was the captain in charge of the arsenal for the Savoca crime family. He would use this opportunity to boost himself to a position that would put him in line to be the Don some day.

Chapter 63

The Senator is Dead

Briggs made a call to Senator Carlson's office. "May I speak to him?" Briggs asked with no particular emotion in his voice.

"Oh, I'm sorry, sir, the senator is not available."

"So when do you think that he will be available, Miss?" This conversation was getting old, and he was getting frustrated.

"I'm afraid that the senator will not be calling you back today, tomorrow or next week," she said with a little bit of sadness in her voice.

"And why is that? Is he out of town or in some secret society that whisks him away at times so the public cannot speak to him?" Briggs was beginning to get abusive.

"No, sir, it's nothing like that. I'm afraid that he's dead. We found him this morning in his kitchen at home around 10:00 AM. When he did not come into work for a 9:00 AM meeting, we sent a security officer to retrieve him, and he found the body."

Danny would need to think through this situation before he contacted Jimmy Garrison.

"What happened to him? Was it a heart attack or something like that?"

"I really can't say. The police have told us that they won't be making a statement until they do some more research and get some answers to more of their questions."

"Thank you," Briggs answered and hung up the telephone.

"Now, this is a wrinkle that I really didn't need," Briggs thought to himself. He knew that now he would need to come up with some new idea of how to get rifles to the Dallas crime family. Jimmy would give him a little time to recover from the change in his supplier, but the mafia really didn't care how he replaced the supplier. They would just expect it to be done in a timely manner.

212

Fortunately, Carlson had spoken of the key player behind the M-16 rifle deal with the Colt Manufacturing Company. It was obvious that Briggs would have to make a trip to Connecticut and ensure that the deal not go sour since Senator Carlson had been removed from the equation.

*   *   *   *   *

"Jimmy, I need to tell you something that you're not going to like," Briggs told his cousin Danny over the telephone.

"Yeah, and what is that, Danny?"

"The key player in my biscuit deal has been found murdered in his apartment. I need to go to D.C. and tidy up things to make sure we don't lose the link that provides us the opportunity to purchase those items. I will get back with you as soon as I have more biscuits ready to ship again." And with that, Briggs hung up and began to figure out how to get things back on track.

Briggs bought an airplane ticket to Washington and made an appointment to speak to Senator Lance Berryman about the deal that he had previously had with him through Carlson. Once he got to the senator's office, he had to wait over thirty minutes before he was ushered into his office.

"So, Mr. Rizzo, is it? How can the great State of Connecticut help you, sir?"

"I think you knew my friend and colleague, Senator Carlson, pretty well, isn't that correct, sir?"

"What does that have to do with you, sir? You mentioned when you made the appointment with my secretary that you needed to speak to me about issues that were very sensitive to my state and my position as senator. Just how does my relationship with the past senator of Maryland have anything to do with those issues?"

"Oh, come on now, Senator. Do you think that Carlson would not have a security back up plan in place in case he was double-crossed in his dealings with you? He shared some things with me that I don't believe you would want exposed to the media about your past." Briggs was bluffing about having specifics about Berryman's shenanigans, but the senator couldn't take the chance that Briggs might have the full story on his exploits. Briggs was betting that Berryman would not take too big a chance that the facts had been passed on to this unwelcomed guest now sitting across from his desk in his office.

"What do you want from me, Mr. Rizzo?"

"Senator Carlson had a deal with you pertaining to a facility down in Dallas, Texas. I think he was trying to get you to increase the shipment to that plant when he met his untimely death. Is that not correct?"

Just who was this man sitting in front of his desk? Berryman gave Briggs a long and pondering stare. He would need to proceed carefully with this guy because he had no idea where Rizzo had gotten these details about his dealings with Carlson. The questions about his ability to cause continuing problems for Berryman were confirmed when Briggs said rather nonchalantly, "I represent a very interested family in Dallas, Texas. Perhaps you have heard of the Savoca family? They have some interests in the restaurant businesses in the Dallas area, and they also are big supporters of the political machine down there. They would appreciate you finding out a way to work with them on this matter. In other words, they are making you an offer that they think you should consider before you reject it. Don Antillo would be inclined to be in your debt if you are able to come through for him on this matter."

Mr. Rizzo rose from his chair and offered his hand in a gesture of friendship as he excused himself to leave the office.

"Here is my business card, Senator. Please give me a call in the next twenty-four hours and let me know if we need to look for another supplier or if we can count on you meeting our new quota." Briggs turned on his heel and left the office.

If there had been any question up to that point whether the Colt Manufacturing Plant would increase its quota to the facility in

Dallas, the matter was settled. Berryman would put that call into the plant as soon as they opened in the morning.

Chapter 64

Putting It All Together

"Klahan, you won't believe what the colonel just told me when I spoke with him on the telephone and brought him up to date on our progress," John said. "He said that the blowhard senator that we both disliked so much in Saigon is dead. It appears from everything that has been found in his apartment that he had been murdered, and there was nothing to indicate that it was anything but a professional hit. Nothing of value appears to have been taken, so they have ruled out a simple breaking and entering, or even a robbery that got out of hand. Also, the colonel said that his sources indicated that a professional hit like this was generally used to 'send a message' to someone else who might be the next target of the killer's wrath. When you consider that he was an active US Senator, the mere fact that he was murdered professionally is so brazen that only a few groups of people would normally be considered suspects."

"What kinds of groups of people was he referring to?"

"Well, for one, the mafia. Although it is not public knowledge at this time, you and I know that Senator Carlson was somehow involved with Briggs. There is no way that Briggs and Carlson would meet out in the open while Briggs is evading the authorities. That is, unless Carlson was involved in Briggs' illegal business transactions. We may never know just how involved the senator was with Briggs, but 'where there's smoke, there's fire.'"

"Now that old saying of yours makes sense—finally!" Klahan said and slapped John on the back. "It's unfortunate that we haven't had time to connect the senator to the weapons that Briggs is obviously procuring and shipping to the mob."

"That's true. But let's get our friends at the CIA and FBI to run down some leads for us and see who else might be a close buddy of the senator and who might have a motive to have him taken out of the equation."

Klahan called their contact at the FBI and asked them if they could find out who Senator Carlos Carlson might have been communicating with in these past few weeks. They hoped that might give them some leads to follow and could even result in leads on who actually killed the senator. In about two hours, they had a return call from the FBI that was very enlightening.

"Here's what we know," the voice on the other end of the telephone line said. "Senator Carlos Carlson had lots of friends in the Senate, but only one where he had a personal interest in the fellow senator's well-being. His name is Lance Berryman, the senator from Connecticut. It appears that Carlson testified in a trial a while back as a character witness and gave the alibi for Berryman in a messy cover-up of possible impropriety that could have brought the senator from Connecticut down. It seems that a pretty young page was suspected of having an affair with Berryman. She was raped and murdered, and Berryman was one of the persons of interest in the case. However, Senator Carlos Carlson rescued his friend and fellow senator with the testimony under oath that Berryman was an upstanding citizen, and that they had been together the very evening the young page was murdered. Berryman was eliminated from the suspect list and the case remains open to this day. It may have nothing at all to do with Carlson's murder, but there is reason to suspect that Berryman was beholding to Carlson, and Carlson could have been blackmailing his friend. Berryman could have had him killed for it. That's a pretty far stretch, but it is a possibility. You would need to get something else more factual than inflammatory rumors on Berryman to subpoena this sitting senator or to question him on either murder."

"Can you tell me if there are any manufacturing plants in Maryland or Connecticut where automatic rifles are made? And also, can you tell me what biscuits have to do with arms trading?"

John and Klahan heard roaring laughter burst from the other end of the telephone, and they just looked at themselves with a troubled and questioning appearance on both of their faces.

"Are you kidding me? Don't you know what biscuits are, John?" The laughter coming from the telephone receiver continued and appeared to increase in intensity.

"No," John said, a little pissed that he and Klahan were being made the butt of someone's joke. "Why don't you tell me?"

"I'm sorry, man. You see, biscuits are considered guns or rifles in 'mob talk', and if you heard monetary prices quoted as well, these are numbers indicating amounts in the hundreds or thousands. The way you can tell if it's hundreds instead of thousands is to practically imagine how much such a weapon would cost on the open market. For instance, ten dollars would indicate a price of one thousand dollars. A biscuit with a price of three dollars would indicate a gun or a rifle with a price of three hundred dollars."

Klahan and John looked at each other and big, beautiful smiles broke out across both of their faces. They began to slap each other on the back and hoot and holler at the top of their lungs.

"It sounds like I said something that pleased you two. Would you care to share your mutual secret that is so satisfying?"

"Absolutely, we will share that fact with you, but first I want to know if there are any rifle manufacturing plants in either Maryland or Connecticut?" John persisted.

It took a minute or two for the analyst on the other end of the telephone line to respond, but when he did, it was like turning on a light in John and Klahan's brains.

"There are a number of small pistol and other handgun manufacturers in both states, but the main manufacturer of weapons in Connecticut is Colt Manufacturing. They manufacture lots of different firearms, but their main bread-and-butter item is the M-16 assault rifle that is exported to Vietnam and to all of our allies in the Middle East."

"Well, I'll be damned!" John said with finality. "That's the key to solving the influx of weapons to the mafia. If you do a little creative thinking, you can assume that Senator Carlson could have been blackmailing Berryman into getting the M-16 rifles sent to the mafia in Dallas. Senator Carlson's decision to remain quiet and to stand by his original statements of Berryman's innocence of the murder of the young page would make Berryman obligated to Carlson in a big way. Who else would have the gall to murder an active senator but another senator? They all believe that they are untouchable and above the law of the land."

"So, how do you want to proceed with this potential sting that you have going on in Dallas? Do you want to bring the local D.A. in on the raid?"

"Hell, no," Klahan burst out before John could answer. "They have done nothing to help us, and they have also tried to stop our investigation. That is why we came to the FBI in the first place. As far as I am concerned, they can read about it in the newspaper like everyone else!"

"Klahan is correct about one thing. If the local government is sympathetic or scared of the local mafia family, then we have no choice but to keep the lid on this investigation until after we raid their offices and storehouses. Are you guys OK with that approach?"

"Absolutely!"

Chapter 65

Tuyen is Happy in Dallas

"Are you enjoying your new life in the United States, Tuyen?" Klahan asked her as she was puttering around the condo dusting and occasionally looking into the kitchen at the meal she was preparing for John and Klahan.

"I like it very much," she replied. "I can walk to the grocery store and the bank without worrying about someone kidnapping me or killing me."

"It makes me happy when you are happy, little Angel," he said and hugged her close to him. Through all of their dealings in Vietnam and here in the US, he had never tried to force a romantic situation on her. He believed that if it was meant to be, then it would happen in its own sweet time. "After all," he thought to himself, "we have the rest of our lives to work out the details."

Those thoughts seemed to fade away as he again thought about relieving John at the listening post near the pizza joint where Jimmy Garrison was supposedly running a money laundering operation out of the back room.

"I will see you after work tomorrow night, Tuyen. We may be tied up until early tomorrow morning."

During all of the maneuvering going on in Dallas with Klahan and John and the constant monitoring that they were doing to try and get more specifics on the mafia's involvement with illicit gun purchases, they never worried about leaving Tuyen alone in the condo for days at a time. It was Dallas, Texas, a city in the middle of the country with a low crime rate overall, albeit the East Dallas area where they lived was much more dangerous than anyone wanted to admit, but she would be fine.

Chapter 66

Let the Raid Begin!

"The first thing that we need to do is to record this mafia captain, Jimmy 'The Hammer' Garrison, talking to Briggs about the next shipment of rifles so we can tie him into the warrant for his arrest as well," John said to the FBI contact in Washington. "Let's see if we get any more specific input from Briggs before we go breaking down doors."

The next two weeks consisted of tapping telephone lines and listening to conversations about whores, money laundering, extortion, illegal gambling, and other major crimes, as well as some minor misdemeanors. Just about the time John, Klahan and the FBI were getting ready to give up on securing more information on the weapons, they got a break.

"Jimmy," the recognizable voice of Danny Briggs pierced the sound in the room, "I've got some good news. There is one more shipment of biscuits coming your way, and then it appears that I have been able to convince the supplier to increase the shipment by 100% as you wished. We had a major disruption with our source of supply, but I think I have repaired the damage. Don't worry, though, because I will stay on top of it until it is successfully handled. Tell your family members that I'm very happy to be their main supplier for these items."

"They will be happy, Danny. I will do my best to support you and explain the difficulties that you have overcome to keep the supply that we need coming, and I know that they will be glad you were able to work through it."

"Thanks, Jimmy, I had to do a little name dropping to convince them that they really didn't have a choice but to continue with the shipments. Otherwise, we would have had to try to renew the old line of supply from Saigon. We really don't want to go back to that situation unless there is no other option."

"OK, Danny, sounds good. Just give me a call when you get the news for me when the shipments will resume, so I can share it with my family members."

*   *   *   *   *

John called the FBI office back as soon as the telephone call between the cousins was over. "Was that enough to get a warrant?"

"Yes, John. Put your combat gear on, because we are going in hot in about an hour. I have alerted the local FBI branch about the task force, and we are set to go. You will need to meet them at Dealey Plaza at 1:00 PM. We have a list of every office, bar, lounge, storage facility and home address of the Savoca Family members in Dallas. The task force will be made up of FBI and local DPS officers. About the time the FBI notifies the DA that we are taking down Jimmy 'The Hammer' Garrison and his goons, we will have most of them in custody. There's no way they can notify anyone of anything because the local DPS will only be notified ten minutes before the raid about the purpose of our search warrants. And by the way, John, we traced the telephone call from your deserter SGT Major Briggs. We have an arrest warrant issued in his name as well, but what may surprise you is that the address is in San Diego, California."

"Let's get this thing underway," shouted the local FBI director. "We will take the pizza parlor where Jimmy 'The Hammer' is supposedly operating, and the rest of you have your lists of places and people that we want arrested. We need to make this a clean takedown, and we need to do it by 2:00 PM. Is everyone ready?"

John and Klahan went with the FBI director to assist with Jimmy Garrison and his soldiers that might be present at the pizza joint. By four o'clock in the afternoon, there were one hundred and fifty-three Savoca Family members in the custody of the FBI. It had been a roaring success.

"So, Lieutenant Bender, tell us how you pulled this off!" One of the local television stations was interviewing a Dallas Police Department officer on the evening news. "Will this help us wipe out the violent crime wave that appears to be overtaking our city? Who were the main people who got this done?" she pried him with questions.

"All I can tell you is that if it were not for two investigators who have been pursuing this criminal activity for about six months, we never would have been able to identify and catch these criminals. I think I heard that they started this investigation from Vietnam or something like that."

As soon as Briggs heard the news about the large number of arrests in the Dallas area, and the seemingly insignificant information about how the investigation started, he put as many clothes in his suitcase as he could pack, started his car, and left his new place of residence for a random hotel in San Diego. He would figure out tomorrow how to evade the unbelievable manhunt that John Bremen and Klahan had continued.

These two need to be taught a lesson. That little wench from Saigon is probably staying with Klahan in Dallas. They are going to pay for this inconvenience. Briggs picked up the telephone and dialed the number that his cousin had given him for a button man in Dallas.

"Jimmy 'The Hammer' told me to give you a call if I needed some work done in the Dallas area. I need for you to look up the address of an individual who is probably renting an apartment in the area. John Bremen is his name, and there may be a young, Vietnamese girl staying with him. She needs to be eliminated, but it needs to look like an accident. I need for you to do this today before five in the afternoon—if possible."

"If Jimmy gave you my number, then you know the routine. I'll expect twenty-five thousand dollars to be wired into my bank account by tomorrow at noon. If you fail to wire the money, I will

223

come looking for you." And with that, the telephone line went dead.

John and Klahan were finishing up with the booking portion of the arrests that had been made that day. The DA had come by and had given them a very somber, disgusting look as he went through the motions of doing his job. It was obvious to them that he was not pleased that they had taken matters into their own hands.

"John Bremen?" the uniformed officer asked his question to no one in particular in the booking room.

"That's me, Officer. What can I do for you?"

"I'm afraid I have some bad news for you. There was an explosion at your apartment complex a little while ago, and there were three units totally destroyed in the fire that persisted after the initial explosion. It appears that your unit was one of the residences that was destroyed."

"Was anyone hurt in the explosion?" Klahan ran over to the officer and asked frantically.

"I'm sorry. It appears a young woman was killed in the explosion. They think it might have been a natural gas accident, but I checked with the apartment manager, and she said the utilities were all electric, so we just are not sure at this point how it happened. We will keep you informed as we learn more about the situation. Please accept my condolences."

*   *   *   *   *

Jimmy Garrison and the Savoca Family members had more friends in the Dallas County Jail than they had on the street.   It wasn't very long until the message was sent along to Jimmy that Briggs would send him a note discretely through a guard who was on the payroll of the Savoca Family giving him some important information about who had ratted him out.

"Mr. Garrison," a guard at the jail said to Jimmy when he was able to isolate him from the other inmates, "I have a note from a

Mr. Rizzo for you. He said it was important to get it to you as soon as possible," and the guard handed the note to him. The note had one name on it, and that name was John Bremen. Jimmy asked the guard for his one telephone call to his attorney, and within a few hours most of the Savoca family was out of jail and on their way home. It was discouraging for the FBI and for John and Klahan. They would continue to make their case for this arrest, but they knew that the Savoca family had a dozen or more lawyers on retainer. What they didn't know was that Briggs had made John and Klahan highly visible to the Savoca family, and that would impact their lives for a long time to come.

Chapter 67

Picking up Briggs' Trail Again

John and Klahan had no idea that they were on the watch list for the Savoca Family, but it probably wouldn't have changed their plans even had they known.

"Klahan, the FBI task force gave us several scenarios of where they think Briggs might be hiding in this area. We have chased him to a neighborhood near Normal Heights. They believe that he has taken a room at the Berkshire Motor Hotel there, and they have it under heavy surveillance and want to know if they should detain or arrest Briggs if they locate him. I told them to arrest him and hold him for us to interrogate."

"That sounds like a good plan to me, John. How soon do they think they can get that done?"

"They indicated that they thought it would happen within the hour."

"Should we take him to a local police station or stay outside of the local law on this one?"

"Let's play it by ear, but I don't want to be restricted to decent behavior with Briggs if he fails to talk to the authorities. I want to beat the info out of him if he doesn't come clean."

Klahan shook his head affirmatively.

*   *   *   *   *

Briggs did come back to the hotel in his automobile but spotted the undercover vehicles camped out all around his room, so he just drove on to another hotel to book a room. Things were heating up, and he was afraid that his ability to give these two guys the slip over and over might be coming to an end.

"There he goes," someone shouted as they saw Briggs drive away from the hotel. "Let's get him, boys." They all canvassed the neighborhood until they found the vehicle that Briggs had been driving earlier that day. It took another two hours canvassing the houses one by one, but they eventually cornered him. Surprisingly, he gave up without a fight.

*   *   *   *   *

"We finally have Briggs in custody, Klahan. How does it feel?"

"I would like it better if they had shot him instead of arresting him. I'm sure he had something to do with the fire and Tuyen's death back in Dallas. That man is evil personified!"

"We need to spend some quality time with the SGT Major before the FBI guys decide to charge him with all of the things that I'm sure they have the capability to do. He's being held down at the county jail until the FBI can arrange a prisoner transport for him back to headquarters in Washington."

"So what's keeping us from having a session with him? You know, the FBI wouldn't have even known about Briggs if we hadn't told them about him back in Nassau."

John picked up the telephone and called the FBI in Washington. After a short conversation with their contact there, John announced, "They are giving us six hours to interrogate him before they whisk him away to Washington. Let's get down there and do our best to get some answers from him before he's taken away."

It was a two hour flight to San Diego from Dallas, and they were in the San Diego FBI office waiting to interview Briggs.

*   *   *   *   *

Thirty minutes later, they were waiting in an interrogation room for Briggs to be brought in and cuffed to a table in front of them. They had been chasing this guy so long, it seemed surreal that they really were going to sit down with him and see what made a criminal mastermind so driven.

"Well, look what we have here," Briggs said as he was escorted into the room and handcuffed to the table. "I have to give it to you guys. You just don't know when it's time to let go or something that's too big for your small minds to comprehend."

"It looks to me that you are the one who has the real issues, SGT Major. We can get up and leave this room and jail any time we want to go home, but you will be calling it home, along with other detention centers, for many years to come," John said.

"Sure, it looks pretty bad for me right now, but things will improve as soon as my high-powered lawyer gets through with these local yokels. You have no idea how much one of those New York attorneys costs these days. It's lucky for me that Don Antillo of the Savoca Family likes me. However, he and his inner circle of friends are not too happy about you causing the delay in their ability to procure M-16 rifles. I'm sure you'll be hearing from them in the near future, as I made sure your names were associated with the problems they incurred in Dallas in that sting you engineered. It was pretty brazen of you to go after one of the five families, John. It was definitely stupid, but brazen none-the-less."

"Look here, you son-of-a-bitch, did you have anything to do with Dao's death in Saigon or the fire in Dallas that killed Tuyen?" Klahan growled.

"Do you think I would admit to premeditated murder either in the US or in Saigon? How stupid do you really think that I am?" He laughed at his own question.

"I don't think you're stupid. You are mentally ill. Anyone who would kill innocent women or their own soldiers for money has to be mentally deranged!" Klahan continued.

"Your troubles are just beginning," Briggs told them. By the time Jimmy Garrison gets through with you, your experience with me will seem like a fairy tale."

"I would worry about myself if I were you, Briggs. The people you will be spending many days and nights with in the future don't particularly like traitors!" John said. As they left the interrogation room, Briggs just smiled that maniacal smile of his.

"There's not much more for me to do here, John," Klahan said as they finished up the paperwork on Briggs' capture and detention. "I think that I will take Tuyen home and bury her in her beloved city of Hua. I know she would be pleased to know that she will be spending eternity next to her family in the area where she grew up as a girl and thrived until the Battle of Hua."

"You were a great help to me, Klahan, and I would have never been able to run Briggs to ground if I hadn't had you as a partner and fellow investigator. I may be calling on you again in the future to help me investigate a case if I stay involved with the CIA until my military hitch is up. Keep in touch with me just in case I need you!" he said with a big smile.

"Absolutely, I will."

"What will you do back in Saigon?"

"Well, I have it on good authority that I can buy back the Magic Fingers Steam and Cream Massage Parlor if I want to do so. Buying it and operating it was the first time in my life that I felt I had complete control of my situation in life. I am thinking of returning and running it in memory of Tuyen. She was a little angel. And what will become of you, John Bremen—or should I say Bill Hicks?"

"I'm definitely in search of an identity, Klahan. Hopefully, I will figure out who I am in time to get out of the military service and begin a new life without so many complications."

"My best wishes and the prayers of my ancient ancestors go with you, John Bremen." Klahan stuck out his hand, shook John's hand vigorously, turned on his heel and walked away.

As John watched this handsome, bright and energetic young man walk out of his life, he knew down in his soul that their paths would probably cross again someday.

Epilogue

SGT Major Briggs was being held at the Federal Detention Center in San Diego when a fire broke out in the facility. Nine hundred inmates at the facility had to be evacuated to local county jails until the buildings were suitable for prisoners again. Miraculously, Briggs was not to be found when all of the inmates were rounded up and resettled in the detention center two weeks later. No one seemed to be able to account for the lack of paperwork that should have followed Briggs to his temporary holding cell. He just seemed to have vanished into thin air.

Jimmy "The Hammer" Garrison was not indicted on any of the charges that were brought against him or any of his family members. There were some irregularities in the search warrants that were issued to the FBI, which made all the information seized by the agents inadmissible in court, so they were released without any charges being made against them. The rumor going around the city of Dallas crime scene was that Jimmy was looking for a guy named John Bremen, who supposedly fingered him for the FBI. Jimmy planned to exact his revenge on this Bremen guy as soon as he was able to find him. It had cost Jimmy and his family over one million dollars in lost revenue, not to mention the embarrassment in the local media when the arrests were made that fateful evening. Yes, John Bremen would learn that it was not a good thing to mess with the Savoca Family.

Only a few months after Danny Briggs was missing from detention, the M-16 rifle sales began again in Dallas. The Colt Manufacturing Company had decided to increase the sales to the Savoca Family, for obvious reasons.

John Bremen decided to resign from the Navy and enter the ninety day training program at the FBI Academy in Quantico, Virginia. He had been given a special discharge that allowed him to basically transfer his military commitment to the FBI. Colonel

Forsett in Saigon had made the recommendation for him, and John was happy to be able to learn some of the more sophisticated techniques that special agents used on a daily basis. He thought it might help him stay alive in the wake of the information that Jimmy "The Hammer" Garrison was gunning for him.

John Bremen wanted to bring Danny Briggs to justice and help the FBI curtail the mafia's gun running business that they were using to gain control of the inner cities in the United States. John Bremen was ready for the ultimate challenge.

Made in the USA
Charleston, SC
17 May 2016